THE LAST DREAM

THE LAST DREAM

PEDRO ALMODÓVAR

TRANSLATED BY FRANK WYNNE

HARPERVIA

An Imprint of HarperCollins*Publishers*

Originally published as *El último sueño* in Spain in 2023 by Penguin Random
House Grupo Editorial, S.A.U.

FIRST HARPERVIA EDITION PUBLISHED IN 2024

Designed by Yvonne Chan

Library of Congress Cataloging-in-Publication Data has been applied for.

ISBN 978-0-06-334976-6

24 25 26 27 28 LBC 5 4 3 2 1

For Lola García,

my brother Agustín,

and Jonás Peiró

And they contained accounts of moments that he treasured but could share with no one. Casual glances at young men who had come to his lectures or whom he encountered at a concert. Glances that were sometimes reciprocated and then became unmistakable in their intensity. While he enjoyed the homage he received in public and appreciated the large audiences he attracted, it was always these chance meetings, silent and furtive, that he remembered. Not to have registered in his diary the message sent by the secret energy in a gaze would have been unthinkable.

—Colm Tóibín, *The Magician*

CONTENTS

INTRODUCTION

I've been asked to write my autobiography more than once, and I've always refused. It's also been suggested that I let someone else write my biography, but I have always felt somewhat resistant to the idea of a book entirely about me as an individual. I've never kept a diary, and whenever I've tried, I've never made it to page two. In a sense, then, this book represents something of a paradox. It might be best described as a fragmentary autobiography, incomplete and a little cryptic. Still, I believe that the reader will end up getting the most information about me as a filmmaker, as a fabulator (as a writer), and the way in which my life makes things blend together. But there are contradictions even in what I've just written: I say I've never kept a diary, and there are four texts here that prove the opposite: one about the death of my mother, one about my visit to the Mexican singer Chavela Vargas in Tepoztlán, the account of a pointless day, and "A Bad Novel." These four texts are snapshots of my life as I was living it, without any degree of distance. This collection of stories (I call everything a story, I don't distinguish between genres) demonstrates the intimate relationship between what I write, what I film, what I live.

The unpublished stories, together with a bunch of others, had been filed in my office by Lola García. Lola is my assistant in this and many other ventures. She compiled them, extracting them from several old blue folders rescued in the chaos of my many moves, and she and Jaume Bonfill decided to dust them off. I had not read them since I first wrote them. Lola had filed them away and I'd forgotten about them. Had she not suggested it, it never would have occurred to me to read them after so many decades. Sensibly, Lola selected a few, to see how I would react to rereading them. In the isolated moments between the preproduction and postproduction of *Strange Way of Life*, I entertained myself by rereading them. I haven't tinkered with them, because what I found interesting was remembering myself and remembering them as they were written at the time and seeing how my life and everything around me changed after I left school with a high school diploma.

I have known that I was a writer since I was a boy, I always wrote. If I was certain about one thing, it was my literary vocation, and if there is one thing about which I'm not certain, it's my achievements. There are two stories about my love of literature and writing ("The Life and Death of Miguel"—written over the course of several afternoons between 1967 and 1970—and "A Bad Novel," written in 2023).

I made my peace with some of them and remembered how and where I wrote them. I can picture myself, in the courtyard of the family home in Madrigalejo, writing "The Life and Death of Miguel" on an Olivetti typewriter under a grapevine with a skinned rabbit hanging from a string, like one of those revolting flycatchers. Or writing on the Q.T. in the Telefónica offices after work, in the early seventies. Or, of course, in the different houses where I've lived, writing in front of a window.

These stories are a complement to my cinematographic works: sometimes they served as an immediate reflection of the moment I was experiencing and either became films many years later (*Bad Education*, certain sequences of *Pain and Glory*), or will end up doing so.

All are texts of initiation (a stage I have not yet finished), and many were born of a desire to escape boredom.

In 1979 I created a character, Patty Diphusa, who is uninhibited in every sense ("Confessions of a Sex Symbol"), and I began the new century with an account of my first day as an orphan ("The Last Dream"), and I would say that in all subsequent writings—including "Bitter Christmas," where I allow myself to include a set piece about Chavela Vargas, whose indelible voice appears in a number of my films—I turn my gaze inward and become the new character about whom

I write in "Adiós, Volcano," "Memory of an Empty Day," and "A Bad Novel." This new character, myself, is the polar opposite of Patty, although we are aspects of a single person. In this new century I've become more somber, more austere, more melancholic, less certain, more insecure, and more afraid, and this is where I find my inspiration. The proof can be found in the films I've made, especially in the past six years.

Everything is in this book. In it, I discover that, when I first got to Madrid in the early seventies, I was already the person I would become: "The Visit" was transformed in 2004 into *Bad Education*, and had I had the money, I would have already made my directorial debut with "Joanna, the Beautiful Madwoman" or "The Mirror Ceremony" before going on to make the films I have made since. But there are some stories written between 1967 and 1970, before I moved to Madrid: "Redemption" and the aforementioned "The Life and Death of Miguel." In both I can sense, on one hand, that I had just left high school and, on the other, my youthful anxieties, my fear of being trapped in a village, and my need to get out as soon as possible and go to Madrid. (During those three years, I lived with my family in Madrigalejo, Cáceres.)

I have tried to leave the stories as I wrote them, but I admit that I could not resist reworking "The Life and Death of Miguel." The style felt too prissy so I have tweaked it a little, while respecting the original flavor. This is one of the stories that surprised me reading it again after more than fifty years. I perfectly remembered the premise, to recount a life in reverse.

That was the essential and, if I may say so, the original idea. Decades later, I thought that *The Curious Case of Benjamin Button* had copied my idea. The story itself is conventional and corresponds to the trajectory of my life, which at that time was very brief. The important thing was the idea. Reading it again now, I see that the story is really about memory and about our powerlessness in the face of passing time. I'm sure I had this in mind when I wrote it, but I had forgotten, and I find it astonishing. My religious education is still present in all the stories from the seventies.

The radical change comes in 1979 with the creation of Patty Diphusa. I could not have written about this character before or after the maelstrom of the late seventies. I picture myself, hunched over the typewriter, doing everything, living and writing, at breakneck speed. The century comes to an end with "The Last Dream," my first day as an orphan. I wanted to include this brief account because I am conscious that these five pages are among the best I have so far written. This does not make me a great writer, which I might be, were I capable of writing at least two hundred pages of the same quality. But, in order for me to write "The Last Dream," my mother had to die.

Besides the relationship between *Bad Education* and "The Visit," these stories contain many of the themes that appear in and shape my films. One is my obsession with Cocteau's *La voix humaine*, which was apparent in *Law of Desire* and was at the origin of *Women on the Verge of a Nervous*

Breakdown; reappeared in *Broken Embraces*; and finally, in 2020, became *The Human Voice*, starring Tilda Swinton. Also in "Too Many Gender Swaps" I talk about one of the key elements in *All About My Mother*: eclecticism, the mixture not only of genders, but of works that marked me. Not simply Cocteau's monologue, but Tennessee Williams's *A Streetcar Named Desire* (El Deseo—*Desire*—is the name of my production company), and John Cassavetes's film *Opening Night*. I have appropriated everything that has ever fallen into my hands or flashed before my eyes and made it my own, without quite reaching the limits of León in "Too Many Gender Swaps."

As a filmmaker, I was born in the midst of the explosion of postmodernism: ideas come from everywhere, styles and periods all coexist, there are no gender prejudices or ghettos. There was no market either, only the desire to live and to do things. It was the ideal breeding ground for someone who, like me, wanted to take on the world.

I could draw inspiration from the courtyards of La Mancha, where I spent my early childhood, or from the dark room of Rockola, pausing, where necessary, in the more sinister areas of my second childhood in the prison-school run by the Salesians. Years that were both turbulent and radiant because the horror of the Salesian school was scored to the Latin masses that I sang as a soloist in the choir (*Pain and Glory*).

I can say now that these were the three places that formed me: the courtyards of La Mancha, where women made bobbin lace, sang, and bitched about everyone in town; the explosive and utterly free nights in Madrid between 1977 and 1990; and the tenebrous religious education I received from the Salesian brothers in the early sixties. All of this distilled into this volume, together with a few other ingredients: desire not merely as the spur and inspiration for my films, but also as madness, epiphany, a law to which one must submit, as though we were characters in the verses of a bolero.

THE VISIT

In the street of a little town in Extremadura, a young woman of about twenty-five grabs the attention of passersby because of her extravagant appearance. It is midmorning, and her getup, in itself flamboyant, seems even more inappropriate in the light of day. But she walks imperturbably, paying no heed to the stares of surprised onlookers. The young woman moves with supreme poise, as though carrying out a long-standing, carefully formulated plan. Her dress, her hat, and her various accessories are identical to those worn by Marlene Dietrich in *The Devil Is a Woman* when she tries to seduce the high-ranking official into giving passports to her and Cesar Romero. More than an impersonation, the woman's movements perfectly embody those of the famous star. In the context of a small town, this sophisticated yet anachronistic spectacle seems utterly surreal and scandalous.

The woman stops outside the door of a school run by the Order of Saint Francis de Sales and then saunters into the building with the same self-possession she displayed walking down the street. Without a flicker of hesitation, she moves as though she is intimately familiar with the school. An astonished priest emerges from the porter's lodge to meet her.

—What can I do for you, señorita? —he asks awkwardly.

—I would like to see the headmaster —the woman says with devastating artlessness. The priest looks at her, half-terrorized, and says without conviction:

—I don't know whether he is here just now.

—I know that he is always in his office at this hour.

Though the young woman's tone is cutting, her confidence defuses any potential provocation elicited by her words. The priest looks her up and down. He does not know what to say. He should not allow her to enter, he thinks, her appearance is positively shocking.

—The thing is, this is a school for young boys, and . . .

—And what?

—Well . . . you . . . in that dress . . .

—What is wrong with my dress? —The young woman glances down as though worried she might find a stain or a tear in the fabric—. Don't you like it?

—It's not that . . .

—Then what is it? Surely you're not telling me that the pupils here have never seen a woman?

—Señorita!

2

She cuts him short:

—Is the headmaster in or not?

—He may not be able to see you right now.

—I have come on a very urgent matter that concerns him as much as it does me. But you needn't trouble to escort me, I know the way. My brother studied here and I often came to visit.

Without waiting for a response, she strides through the narrow passageway leading to the courtyard. The priest, alarmed, chases after her.

—Señorita! Señorita!

—It's over there, the door on the left, isn't it?

—Yes, that's the one. —The dazed priest watches as she disappears.

The courtyard is deserted, today is a holiday so most of the boarding students are out on the town. The few still in the school are bookworms or those in detention. The young woman ostentatiously descends the stairs leading from the courtyard and heads toward the door indicated by the priest. She gives two or three curt raps and waits.

—Come in —calls a voice from inside. Seeing her enter, the monk of about forty-five seated behind the desk cannot conceal his amazement.

—And who might you be?

—Don't look at me like that. —The woman smiles confidently—. I'm the sister of one of your former pupils, and I've come to talk to you on his behalf.

3

The headmaster addresses her timorously, though he is curious to know what this is about.

—Which pupil are you talking about?

—I'm the sister of Luis Rodríguez Bahamonde.

Hearing the name, the monk's expression changes and he looks at the young woman more intently, paying no attention to her appearance, looking only for some resemblance that will convince him that what she says is true.

—So, you're Luis's sister? —he says excitedly.

The woman nods coldly.

—I was a great friend of your brother. He was not just another pupil to me. —The monk's words are tinged with evident nostalgia.

—I've come to talk to you about him.

—Well, I'm delighted! It's so long since I last saw him! We were good friends . . . but when the boys leave the school, they forget us. I wrote to him once or twice to see how he was doing, but he never wrote back. How is he? I suppose he's changed a lot, he'd be a grown man now. Looking more closely, I see a lot of him in you. You have the same eyes.

The woman listens, serious and silent.

—Obviously, given my vocation I never had children myself, but I feel the same duty as any man to protect and educate those starting out in life. —He pauses for a moment. The young woman is staring at him, her eyes never blinking, but he scarcely notices, so engrossed is he in his memories—. Your brother Luis was like a son to me. I am so happy that you're here. What is your name?

—Paula.

—I have so many things I want to know. But first, tell me what brings you here.

—I have some bad news.

—What happened?

—Some months ago, my parents died in a car crash.

—Oh, that's dreadful. I'm so sorry.

The headmaster looks genuinely upset. Ever since Paula stepped into his office, he has been trying to ignore her bizarre outfit. He was so delighted by the thought that she was Luis's sister . . . Now that he has heard about her parents' deaths, and given the icy way in which she relayed the news, her manner seems utterly incomprehensible, particularly her gaudy, deeply inappropriate clothing. In order not to make the situation worse, he makes a valiant effort and bites his tongue, and this restraint saps from the conversation the warmth he hoped to convey.

—As you can imagine, it's been a terrible blow —Paula continues—. The past few months have been unbearable. But now I'm starting to recover the strength to fight.

From Paula's lips, as she stands, sheathed in her opulent dress, the words ring false, but their decisiveness brooks no objection.

—God will help grant you succor. Trust in Him, you are not alone.

The two remain silent for a moment, then the priest asks:

—And Luis, how has he taken it?

—He was with them, no one survived.

—Oh, my God! Luis!

For the monk, this is the worst news he could have imagined. He sits, frozen, at his desk, staring wild-eyed at Paula, yet it is not her he sees, but Luis. As he repeats the boy's name, his eyes well with tears. Paula, stony-faced, looks at him impassively. A few moments pass.

—I'm sorry. I cared deeply for your brother. I couldn't have loved him any more if he had been my own son. I watched him grow and mature. This is tragic. How old was he?

—Twenty-four.

The headmaster is devastated. The news has come as a terrible shock. He glances back at Paula. With each passing minute, her clothes seem more outlandish and inappropriate. Moreover, he is irritated by the curt, cold way she is talking about the tragedy. How can she seem so utterly indifferent while telling him her parents and her brother are dead? Paula sits facing him. She seems above it all, as though even death cannot touch her. What is she hiding behind this mask of arrogance?

—I brought you one of the last photos of him. I thought you might like to keep it.

—Oh, yes, of course.

At the outset, the headmaster felt that it was best not to show how deeply he felt about his former pupil until he got to know Paula better, but he needed to talk about Luis so desperately that he had made no effort to temper his comments. Looking at the boy's sister, he realizes his mistake. Although at the end of the day he has told her nothing that he had not already told the boy's parents when they came to visit Luis. But they reacted very differently. They were proud that their son was under the wing of the most important man in the school.

Now, faced with the terrible news and Paula's icy manner, the monk feels traumatized and uncertain.

—Here —she says—, it was taken shortly before the accident.

It is one of the best photos of Luis's later years. He is naked, the photo showing him from the navel upward. Luis stares out of the photograph as though trying to express his secrets without saying a word. It occurs to the priest that he frequently asked the boy to send him a photo, but he never did.

—He's changed a lot, but if I'd bumped into him on the street, I would have recognized him. I can't believe he's dead.

Paula responds to the priest's grief with sarcasm:

—But I suppose death is not as tragic for you as it is for the rest of us.

—How do you mean? —The headmaster does not understand.

—You have God on your side, and that must be a great comfort. I imagine that for priests, tragedy takes on a very different significance.

The headmaster looks at her as though about to protest, but he bites his tongue.

—Despite our Christian ministry, we are not immune to human suffering —he snaps, feeling irritable and depressed, but he manages not to explode and tell this shameless slut a few home truths—. But let's not talk about that now. Tell me about your brother, what he did in the past few years, what he was like . . .

—He devoted most of his later years to literature. That was what most interested him. He had no confidence in his work, and it's true that he still had a lot to learn, but he'd already written some very interesting things, even if he wasn't very satisfied with them. We loved each other very much —Paula continues, her expression cold, but harder—. We grew up together, I knew him as well as I knew myself, we had no secrets from each other. I came here because I'm sure he would have liked to.

Paula carries on, calm but relentless. There seems to be a veiled threat in everything she says. The headmaster feels nervous, is unsure what tone to adopt. As time passes, the atmosphere becomes strained and he does not know what to do to avoid exacerbating it, because all he wants is for this woman to talk to him about Luis. But, just then, Paula takes out a lipstick and a mirror, and before the priest's astonished eyes, she sensually applies the lipstick. Faced with this grotesque provocation, the priest cannot contain himself.

—Señorita, don't you think it's a little too much?

—A little too much? —She pauses and looks at him.

—All this frivolity.

Paula smiles warmly.

—Oh, I *adore* frivolity.

—Why did you dress like that to come see me? Aside from being out of fashion, it's ridiculous.

The woman seems unsurprised by the abrupt, unpleasant turn the conversation has taken, and continues to be assertively confident.

—Of course, you're a monk, so everything from the outside world must seem salacious.

—I have no idea what this is all about.

The priest no longer makes any attempt to hide his disgust.

—I'll explain why I'm wearing this dress —she says solicitously, as though about to tell a story—. There is a famous movie star, Marlene Dietrich, have you heard of her?

—No —says the priest grudgingly, wondering where exactly this madwoman is going with this.

—I am a huge fan of Dietrich. In one of her old films, she wears a dress exactly like this, and later in the film she sings something like . . .

Paula gets to her feet and sings. The priest tries to interrupt, begs her to be quiet, but she pays him not the slightest heed and carries on until the end, treating him as one member of an invisible audience she must enchant.

—Enough! —mutters the helpless headmaster, who is losing his mind—. Stop this ridiculous performance!

9

Paula smiles maliciously.

—This is only the beginning!

—Why did you come here?

—To talk about my brother —she says, as though nothing had happened—, and to do what he could not do because he did not get the time.

—And was it really necessary to come dressed like this?

—Yes.

—Let me tell you that, but for Luis's memory, I would not have allowed you to say a word.

—The feeling is entirely mutual. I don't particularly like the way you dress either, but I have not mentioned it.

—You look like a prostitute.

—Well spotted . . .

—I don't know your intentions, but I've tolerated you long enough. Get out of my office!

—Don't you want to know about my brother? What happened to your curiosity? Let's be civil. —She waves for him to sit down—. I'm going to read you some of his stories. I assume they would interest you. It was here that he first started writing, I remember. I still have a poetic essay devoted to the Sacred Heart, for which he received an excellent grade in literature. He would have been in the first year of his *bachillerato* at the time.

—Ah, yes, I remember it well. —The priest looks as though he is being shaken like a rag doll—. I taught him literature. He had an extraordinary sensitivity for a boy his age. I'm glad he never stopped.

—As I said, it was his principal occupation. A book of his selected short stories is about to be published. It is still at the printer, but I brought you an advance copy.

—This whole thing is absurd! Were it not for your uncanny resemblance, I would have thought it was a joke in poor taste. But, despite the circumstances, I am grateful to you for taking the trouble to bring me his writings. I will read them with pleasure.

—I am going to read the first couple aloud. They deal with his time here at school.

—Does he mention us?

—Yes, listen.

Every month, the most diligent pupils—I was almost always one of them—were rewarded with a day off, while the other boys had to stay in school and attend their usual classes. If it was not too cold, we would spend the whole day in the countryside, leaving immediately after breakfast and returning in time for dinner. On such occasions, we were always escorted by a teacher. Most of the teachers considered it a reward too, since they had as much fun as we did. Their only responsibility was to keep an eye on us and ensure nothing happened. Often, the success of these outings depended entirely on the teacher in charge. Some would plan an itinerary, filled with original, entertaining activities. Another used to endlessly regale us with amusing anecdotes and we could never tell whether they were true, whether they were made up on the spot, or whether he had read them in a book, though he always swore that they had all happened to him.

On the particular day I am going to relate, we were accompanied by Don Ceferino, a priest who was about thirty. It was a beautiful spring day and we went to a nearby mountain, next to a river and some woodland. I didn't really trust Don Ceferino. He had a certain worldly sophistication that made me keep my distance. I was very pious, and to me, the typical priest was the figure we read about in biographies, a man always about to pray, a man whose eyes were ever fixed on the heavens. The fact that Don Ceferino smiled like an average man made me think that there was something about him unsuited to his vocation.

I don't know how, but I found myself lying next to him on a hillside, in the shade of a tree, in the shelter of the bushes, while the other boys were playing somewhere on the hill. They must have been nearby, but we could not see them. (Only now do I understand just how reckless Don Ceferino was, one of the boys could have reappeared at any moment.) I can't remember what exactly he was talking about, but it was something that did not matter to either of us. He simply talked in order to fill the silence. He opened a number of the buttons of his cassock, the ones just around his waist, then grabbed my hand and slipped it inside so I could grope him. Trembling with fear and excitement, I instantly withdrew my hand, but he brutally grabbed it.

After a pointless struggle I allowed him to use my hand to masturbate himself, feeling simultaneously curious and disgusted. The hair around his penis reminded me of the feel of dry grass in a meadow. Back at school, I could not comprehend what had happened. To allay my fears, I decided to talk to my spiritual director. I could think of no one else I could turn to and tried to convince myself that he would help.

The following day, after lunch, I went to his room to speak with him. I knocked on the door and from inside he asked who I was and what I wanted. When I told him I wanted to make confession, he said that he was busy and told me to come to evening confession, during benediction (benediction was a religious service we attended every day before dinner). At that time, I was deeply insecure about life. I felt helpless and sought refuge in religion, although it did not entirely fulfill me. But I was so young (ten years old) that, even though I did not feel any religious faith, I managed to persevere. At that time, the conviction that I was in a state of mortal sin was excruciating. The hours before nightfall seemed to drag on forever. I felt as though God would strike me down at any moment. It seemed to me completely logical that I could be struck by lightning, or hurled down a staircase by some invisible force, or that the whole school would collapse and bury me.

When at last we went into the chapel, I thanked God that I was still alive, and my terror was assuaged by the sight of

13

the confessional booth. I rushed over and knelt down for a moment to examine my conscience, but I could not concentrate. I went to the front of the confessional and lifted the little curtain that hid the priest so I could put my head in. I assumed that, as always, he would put an arm around my shoulder the better to hear me, and there, embraced and cloaked by the curtain, he would whisper the customary phrases, but that is not what happened. Seeing me in front of him, he turned on the light and . . . I don't know how to describe what I felt. There was my spiritual director, Father José, smiling at me, dressed as a woman, wearing a forties-style red velvet suit and a blond wig. The makeup accentuated his usual paleness and flushed his cheeks, his lips were a veiny red. I could not muffle a cry.

—Don't be scared —he said, in dulcet tones.

—It's just that I didn't expect to see you like this, Father. —My mind was reeling.

As though oblivious to my terrible bewilderment, he said very simply:

—Do you like it?

I could not form a single word. And he explained to me professorially:

—Beauty is a gift from God, so to cherish beauty is to cherish God. And all this artifice adds to my beauty, does it not? The importance of our ministry does not depend on how we dress. It is not true that the robes make the monk. The essence of what it means to be a priest is something intimate, abstract, which has nothing to do with material accessories. I have done this not merely because I find it amusing, but so that I may open your mind and you will be more lenient in judging the behavior of others. Is that clear?

—Yes, Father.

I felt even more confused.

—What I am doing here is an act of charity, a demonstration of my love for my neighbor. I am offering you beauty, and beauty is important, is it not?

—Yes, Father.

—I offer it as a gift to you, and to me, and it gives us both pleasure. That is not to say I shall always dress like this, though there is no law forbidding it. Since the monks in my order traditionally don black cassocks, I shall respect the judgment of our founding father. It is important that you understand that in our life, there will be many different stages and sometimes it is amusing to dress differently. Now, I shall hear your confession. I'm going to put on my stole.

He spoke the usual phrases, but after I said:

—Bless me, Father, for I have sinned —I was so confused that I did not know how to begin.

—Come, tell me, how have you sinned?

—Well . . . I don't know how to explain it. Something horrible happened to me, and I'm not sure, but I think I may have given in to temptation, although at the time what I actually felt was disgust.

Nervously I told him what had happened at the picnic.

—The thing that differentiates us from the animals, my dear Luis, is that we can give way to temptation. We are capable of sin because we have the free will to choose.

—What are you trying to say? I don't understand.

—That what Father Ceferino did is human, and it is understandable. —He smiled calmly.

—Maybe, but it scared me. I didn't sleep at all last night. I had terrible nightmares where everyone was trying to grab me. And I was worried about hell, if something happened to me, I wouldn't be in God's grace . . . because it's a mortal sin, isn't it?

—My son, any human action has no absolute value, it depends on so many things! What happened to you may or may not have been a sin.

—But what about the sixth commandment?

—The commandments are meant for those who intend to sin. Many people need to sin in order to feel important. Just as we have chosen to devote our lives to God, others, on the contrary, do everything possible to make their lives a continuous insult to our Maker. God, as a loving Father, takes care of all of us. We are all His children. Just as we have ways to worship Him, others have ways to offend Him. But if, in your actions, you do not intend to offend God, there is no sin, because your actions have another purpose. At the picnic, Father Ceferino wanted to show you that he was attracted to your body, and you should be flattered. It has nothing whatsoever to do with the sixth commandment.

—I don't understand what you're trying to say —I stammered.

—Yes, yes, you are still a child, but for that very reason we must try to instill in you the true meaning of life. Your parents have entrusted you to our care so that we might educate you, and that is what we do. Through education, you discover the meaning of things, and any new discovery is always confusing. I understand that you are finding all this difficult, but it is our duty to put you in touch with the true values of our existence.

Not only did my spiritual director not reassure me, as I had hoped, but he plunged me into an even more unfathomable abyss. I felt completely alone, unable to fight off the nightmares that plagued me incessantly. I could not talk to anyone about what had happened, the whole world had turned against me. The pupils and the teachers were completely at ease in that hell, they were utterly unaffected by it, and their placidity was a threat to me.

—Here endeth one of the chapters dedicated to the school. What did you think? —Paula says, stone-faced.

The priest is so furious he cannot speak.

—Aren't you delighted that a former pupil immortalized your school and its subtle methods of deformation, as Luis did?

The priest tries to find strength in the hatred he feels for the person sitting opposite him. He does his best to pretend that he is not afraid of her.

—Where are you going with this?

—This has nothing to do with me. I merely represent my brother, your darling Luis.

—Shut up, you disgust me!

—Don't you insult me, you son of a bitch!

—You said it yourself, you're a whore. How can one insult a woman who makes sin her profession, her driving force?

—And what do you call the depravity that takes place in this school under your watch? I give my body to the men who desire me, to those who willingly seek me out, but at the age of ten, what weapons did Luis have to fight you off? You not only violated his body, but you warped his spirit, you sowed chaos and fear. And all in the name of God.

—Shut your mouth! I don't believe Luis wrote a word of that drivel!

—The minister of God has lost his temper —Paula interrupts, angry and mocking—. Why so, if my insults are so hackneyed, if you are so exalted and I so vile?

She pauses briefly so she can carry on with bitter fury.

—Luis died cursing you all, and I have come to avenge him! He did not have the time to do it himself.

The priest looks at her in horror.

—You will not be able to convince me as you did my parents of the purity of the love you felt for him. —Then, mimicking the priest, she echoes his words—: I love him as though he were my own son. —She sniggers—. Bastard! And my parents were so pleased that the headmaster took such a tender interest in their son's education! Poor Luis! I was so young then that he could not confide in me either. Imagine how he felt when he left here! He thought he was insane. The nightmares that tormented him are engraved in this book, captured in that last moment, just as he had freed himself of them. So I have brought them to you and your cohorts, back to the place from which they came, so that you can admire your handiwork.

—You're mad! —the priest shrieks, backed into a corner—. You've come here to insult me! I don't believe that Luis wrote that, I don't believe that you're his sister, I don't believe that he's dead!

He is almost sobbing as he says this.

Abruptly, Paula's tone changes. She is suddenly calmer, as though nothing has happened. One way or another she is mistress of this situation.

—I'll read another story. Luis's time at this school was one of the periods of his life that marked him most. You feature in this story.

The priest is about to protest, but he feels cornered. At this point he can no longer throw Paula out onto the street, nor can he stop her starting the second story, because, aside from the fact he has nothing he can use against her, he wants to know what Luis thought of him. Luis, the pupil who, despite everything he says in his story, the priest truly loved.

And Paula begins reading.

Preparations for the festival in honor of Reverend Father the headmaster were already underway two months before it was set to take place. It was a tour de force, all of us pupils and teachers gave our best. I had to neglect my studies a little because I was involved in a lot of the events being prepared for the celebration. There were all kinds of competitions, and the mass, the heart of any religious event, was the longest and most brilliant of the school year. I was the soloist in the choir. There were also plays, poetry recitals, sporting events, etc. One of the main reasons the pupils were excited was the special food we were to be served that day, which, together with the sporting final, was the most joyous event, and the highlight of the festival. I wasn't lucky enough to really enjoy this part. I had to eat quickly and was immediately escorted to the monks' dining hall, which was separate from ours. It was a privilege for a pupil to be allowed into the dining hall, especially on an occasion when I was to be one of the stars of the evening.

When I stepped inside, I couldn't believe my eyes. The dining hall was dominated by a huge painting of Christ wearing the crown of thorns. Although the subject was religious, the treatment surprised me. It was a half-length portrait, with Christ depicted in three-quarter profile, his head slightly raised and his shoulders forward. His lips were parted, like Marilyn's in Warhol's famous pictures, in an expression of mingled pleasure and pain. The crown of thorns was fastened and buried into his flesh just below his shoulders, pinioning his arms against his torso. His shoulders appeared above this girdle of thorns. From around the thorns spouted thin trickles of blood, like tassels.

The monks sat around the long table like the apostles at the Last Supper. I was even more stunned by another idiosyncrasy in their appearance: the monks were wearing stunning cocktail dresses. One was dressed in 1920s flapper style, another in the black, existentialist style of Juliette Gréco. There was one in a flamenco gown with a long train and kiss curls at the temples. Another was dressed as Cleopatra, another as a movie star with feathers and a sequined bikini, and so on. The dining hall looked like a great masked ball. I felt intimidated by their joyousness, because it was not just that their clothes were different. The monks were behaving in a way I did not recognize. I could never have imagined that the men who treated us with sadistic cruelty could be so jolly and boisterous in other circumstances. I stood, dumbfounded, marveling at this curious display of opulence and frivolity.

Truth be told, they were funnier and more beautiful than when they wore their black cassocks, but the drastic change in their behavior shook my mind, which was already feeble and vulnerable. They treated me with the same dizzy exuberance I remember from my older sister's friends, when, before going to a party, they would be putting the finishing touches to their outfits at my house while I watched, spellbound. One even kissed me, leaving his crimson lipstick on my cheek. I realized this only much later, and was filled with shame.

Before my performance I was given nougat, caramels, and other candies. I felt completely overwhelmed. I didn't know how to react and scolded myself that I couldn't behave naturally, but they not only understood my discomfort, they were amused by it, and this made things even more difficult for me.

The great moment had arrived. A hush fell over the room and one of the monks got to his feet. Like everyone else, his eyes glistened with joy and alcohol. He said what was customary in any kind of homage:

—I shall be brief because the songs and spectacles that await us are more entertaining than anything I can say. —He glanced at the headmaster—. On behalf of all those present, I would like to pay tribute to the man who, with the Lord's help, so fittingly governs this school. I hope that this little soirée will serve to highlight our loyalty and our devotion. To this end, the charming Luis will entertain us with a repertoire of songs, chosen from among our dear headmaster's favorites.

Standing in the center of the dining hall, I began my performance, excited by the warmth of the atmosphere. Before I sang, I introduced the first song:

—We all know that the Father Director likes the popular Italian song "Torna a Surriento." I will be singing a version with lyrics penned by Father Venancio, dedicated especially to our director.

From his place at the center of the table, the Father Director looked at me. "Torna a Surriento" had become "Gardener." It went like this:

> O Gardener, O Gardener,
> among the flowers you spend your days,
> making their bright colors blaze
> with the pure flame of your love.
> You give to every tender petal
> the sweet caress of your desire,
> and gaze on heaven, eyes afire,
> wherein your dreams and wishes settle.
> And from your blazing, budding blooms
> sepals and stamens all ablaze,
> there radiates a gentle haze
> that shrouds you in its perfume.
> Continue, then, to till the sod
> and cultivate these precious flowers
> bestowed upon your happy hours
> by our Almighty God.

The following day he summoned me to his office to congratulate me and tell me that he would be going away for a few days. He asked permission to kiss me goodbye, and I just shrugged. He came over and hugged me tightly. I was trembling, I found the whole scene disgusting, though I was also disturbed that under his cassock he was clearly aroused. He started by kissing me on the cheek, then immediately, under great stress, moved on to my lips, and I thought he would never pull away. I felt like a rag doll in his hands.

Paula stops reading. There is a heavy silence in the office. The headmaster does not know what to say, perhaps because, through Luis's words, he has relived every moment of this scene or perhaps because in that moment he wants to rail against these accusations but finds that he does not know how. The second story has left him utterly crushed. On the desk, among the papers and writing materials, there is a letter opener. Unable to control himself, the priest hurls himself at Paula and plunges the letter opener into her chest. The young woman falls to the floor, as blood spreads over her beautiful dress. At the sight of it, the priest's fury is appeased. Some of the papers Paula was holding flutter around her. Luis's memory is with her on the floor, in the pages from which she has just read.

—Dear God, what have I done? —says the priest, panic-stricken.

—I hate you —Paula stammers, and her voice is now a man's.

The headmaster does not know what to do. He tries to undress her so that he can help her, if that is still possible. He dares not call anyone, but he cannot let the woman bleed to death without trying to help. Eventually, he decides to call the priest at the porter's lodge. While he waits, he unbuttons the top of Paula's dress. The letter opener is embedded in her breast. After a last "I hate you," Paula lies completely still. The priest rips off her bra so he can press his ear next to her heart and, holding it in his hand, discovers it stuffed with wadding soaked in blood. Paula's chest is that of a young man. Finally, the demented headmaster understands the purpose of this visit.

—Oh, Luis!

Loudly, he begins to weep over the corpse.

—Luis, Luis! I have killed you . . .

He tries to wipe away the makeup using the wadding from the bra, but succeeds only in smearing the face with blood. He removes the wig and the earrings. What was Paula now looks grotesque, but the priest can see past the blood and makeup. Like a curious Pietà, he takes Luis in his arms. Unable to cradle the whole body as he would like, he kisses him over and over, calling his name like a man possessed.

And this is how the priest from the porter's lodge finds him when he bursts into the office.

TOO MANY GENDER SWAPS

The Second Streetcar

I was admitted to the hospital for a single night, a catheter extending from my penis as far as a drainage bag that collected my sangría-red urine, after an operation for a kidney stone. León was determined to come with me. I asked him not to (I was grateful, obviously), because having him by my bedside would be distracting. The hospital staff recognized him, more from his movies than from the theater, so his presence was highly conspicuous. But León never passed up the opportunity to demonstrate his generosity, which was slightly melodramatic, like everything he did with excessive pleasure, except for acting. Only when acting did he not overact.

"It's something you have to learn to live with," he said, referring to spending a night in the hospital. I assume he was referring more to his experience as an actor than as a human being. León was always an actor. The best and worst things he did in his life were related to performing: the characters he longed to embody, the plays he wanted for himself even if it meant reworking the original to the point of utterly distorting it. The impossible mixture of subjects, a wildly postmodern, irreverent, and violent energy he needed to push himself as an actor and inhabit characters and writers that were sometimes an unnatural fit. His transgressive spirit was a combination of vanity, rebelliousness, and his disregard for others as a general rule. This cocktail made him a fascinating and terrifying character for a director like me, who was also his lover.

A slavish, passionate lover who lived through the early years of our careers as though under a spell, because when León got it right (and he often did), the experience was indescribable. And it was still fascinating and intimidating to see him, twenty-five years older and fifty pounds heavier, in our restaging of *A Streetcar Named Desire*. It was impossible to tell León that, however fascinated he was by the character of Blanche DuBois, he did not have the appropriate physique or gender to play her onstage.

—Why are you talking about gender? —León complained—. When have we ever cared about gender? We'll call him Blanco del Bosque. I'll lose a bit of weight and fuck that brute Kowalski. If Tennessee could see it, he'd be thrilled to finally have a guy fuck Kowalski. It's a lot more humiliating for the character than having fucked delicate little Blanche. I always imagined Kowalski would end up screwing some guy during one of his drunken binges.

In this version, Blanco would be Stella's beloved brother, for whom she feels weakness and compassion. He shows up unexpectedly, depressed, after a long stretch in prison. Blanco had been a brilliant high school math teacher, until he fell from grace, committing a crime that has a terrible reputation even among criminals. Stella knows about the dubious episode for which he was sentenced to prison, but still worships her brother, who is also on the brink of destitution. But, try as they might to hide the facts, Kowalski ends up discovering Blanco's crime, how he abused a boy and ended up behind bars.

Against all odds, and after attempting to convince León that we could be very bold as long as we didn't fall into the grotesque, I got down to work and adapted T. Williams's drama so that a 198-pound, forty-five-year-old León could play Blanche DuBois, without dressing in drag. It was a challenge for both of us.

In the end, the presence of Blanco was as disturbing, almost more so, as that of Blanche. León did lose some weight, because his character was ill when he was released from prison, and by shedding a few pounds he recovered some of his sex appeal. His experience of prison had made him hard. Physically he exuded a seductiveness as animalistic as Kowalski's but darker. He longed to toss the sweaty macho brute out of the house with his gang of cronies so he could be alone with his sister Stella to take care of her baby.

And, once again, León did it, under my direction and with a text I never thought I could write. León provoked, he dazzled, he surprised and transfixed as he had done at the beginning of his career in Marlowe's *Edward II*, our first play together: at the age of twenty, an utterly unknown León, radiating tenderness and malevolence in equal measure, proved to be overwhelming playing the son of the butcher who drives the king mad with love, just as he did with the audiences at the María Guerrero Theatre and me, who shared not only the joy of success with him but the passion that devoured us each night after the play. And after *Edward II* came his first *Streetcar*, playing Kowalski.

For those who had known him since that start to his career, the second *Streetcar* was a metatheatrical show in which they witnessed a conversation between the León of twenty-five years ago and the delirious León-Blanco-Blanche of today, as strong and arrogant as the Polack, but more intelligent, with a mixture of fatal femininity and masculinity that disarmed all those around him. I don't know if the show was very true to Tennessee Williams, I suspect not. Gone was the lyricism of a female Blanche, withered and mad, but the family tragedy exploded into a more brutal, more sinister, more contemporary piece, with hints of Jean Genet. Genet was a sauce we sometimes used to douse our work together.

León was ecstatic. Late triumphs are the ones you savor

most intensely. With early triumphs, you don't have time and you don't realize how hard it will be to have another.

After Blanco del Bosque, I was exhausted. It had worked, but as both director and writer, I was forcing things. I didn't think I could keep up the pace León demanded of me. After twenty-five years of excess, his extravagances sometimes struck me as pathetic and grotesque, and I no longer knew what to do. I had lost that skill, that power. I had also lost the motivation to continue twisting texts so they would fit the actor I loved and admired. I suppose that in losing my passion for León I also lost my talent for writing and directing him.

A few months after the second *Streetcar*, I could see things were coming to an end, but I didn't know when I would have the energy to leave him. Before a dictator is ousted or dies a natural death, the oppressed people can wait for years, with champagne chilling in the fridge to celebrate when the dictator dies. Years of internalizing the change and quietly preparing for when the moment comes. That's how I felt, I had to leave León.

Are You Seriously Asking Me If I'm Alright?!

A few years after the first *Streetcar* we watched *L'Amore*, a thirty-minute short film directed by Rossellini, on television. It was a cinematic adaptation of Jean Cocteau's *La voix humaine*, starring Anna Magnani. It had driven me wild the first time I saw it as a teenager. León had only ever read it, but seeing the role played by Magnani reminded him that he had always had a soft spot for the play.

I was surprised to find I was less enthusiastic on seeing it a second time. Magnani still brimmed with talent and fragility (an actress often characterized by the opposite). It was impossible not to be moved by her, but the play, filmed with slender means, had not stood the test of time. Cocteau's text felt dated. It is something that can happen even to great writers. Sixty years after it was written, there were no women as submissive as the one played by Magnani, no woman could identify with her. I shared my thoughts with León, but he didn't pay me any heed, he was too excited thinking up ideas.

—What could we do with this play?

—Nothing, that's what we're going to do —I said.

—Ever since I read it, I've felt a special connection, and now, after seeing it, the bond is even stronger. When I feel this way, I have to do something about it —said León, and then added—, It's a feeling I recognize very well. I live for it.

—The phone call could be between two men. Men suffer just as much when they're dumped —I suggested—. Obviously, it would need to be adapted, but you can do the monologue, if that's what you mean. The problem is that you'd need to find at least two other monologues to stage a show lasting an hour and a half —I added, just to have something coherent to say—. Or do you want to make a short film?

—A short? No. A feature film. Surely you can think of something?

—To get to ninety minutes would mean creating an extra hour of text. And that strikes me as too much for additional material.

—It's just a matter of writing it, but you need an idea . . . something beyond Cocteau.

—It takes a lot more than an idea —I said—. It's not about padding things out, it's about creating. If the monologue comes at the end of the film, we'd need to create the first hour, leading up to the phone call. It could be set, say, forty-eight hours before the phone call. Show the world of the protagonist during those desperate hours. What he did in those two days before the phone call.

—Two days of waiting with his bags packed, that's a lot of hours. He'd have to be having a breakdown —says León.

This kind of preliminary conversation broadly gives an idea of the spirit and the dynamics of our creative process, which I would then sit down and write alone.

We improvised, or rather, I improvised:

—The character can't stay in the apartment for two whole days. He goes out, looks for his lover, can't find him, but he discovers things he didn't know. That there was a woman in his life, a woman he married and with whom he has a son.

—Yes, but I don't want it to be a story about queers. The lover is bisexual. I'd be the only long-term relationship he's had with a guy, a detour in his sex life.

—You're so behind the times, León! At this point are you actually worried that it might be a story about queers?

—Two men can love each other without being queer. I'm interested in people's passions, I don't give a damn about sexuality or gender.

—I see.

—If he's going to go out and roam the streets meeting other characters, I'd prefer it if they were women. The lover is bisexual. We need to dramatize the fact that he's bisexual, nobody's done that before. Bisexuality is the great neglected topic of the sexual revolution. The fact that the lover is bisexual is doubly frustrating for my character. He has the worst parts to the male lover and the female lover, which only makes his partner more insecure, since he knows he can't fulfill all his fantasies . . .

I didn't take León's personal analysis of bisexuality seriously, but I didn't tell him that. The machine had already begun to grind into action.

—If we want more characters, all we need to do is open the door of the character's apartment —I said.

—How?

—We put it up for rent. He can't bear to carry on living in their little love nest. Everything reminds him of the man who isn't there, in fact it's a miracle he doesn't torch the house. This way, he can meet the most varied characters. He could even meet his lover's son, who comes to view the place with his girlfriend, or even his lover's former wife. He could also meet up with a colleague who's on the run from the police because . . . she's having an affair with a terrorist . . . That's funny.

—An ensemble comedy? I don't know if I want other characters to be funny.

—Your character gets involved in other people's problems and through them he finds salvation.

—I've never played a compassionate character. I don't think I'd be good at it.

—He won't be good-natured, he'll be hysterical. Think Cary Grant or Jack Lemmon. He helps other people out of pure hysteria, because he can't stop.

—You're forgetting about the phone call.

—That's true. We don't need it anymore —I said, surprised at this late realization.

—But what about Cocteau?

—We don't need him. Besides, we'd have to pay for the rights. The basics are the same, a woman . . .

—A man, for fuck's sake!

—A man, who's not gay, but who's madly in love with another man, who's not gay either. The circumstances don't stop them living a life of marital bliss for years. Like Cary Grant and Randolph Scott, they shared a bachelor pad, woke up and slept together, but Hollywood decreed that they weren't gay.

—Don't beat around the bush.

—Cocteau's premise remains: a man, waiting for his lover to come and pick up his suitcases. And a dog who shares his grief at being abandoned by his master. With this and the people coming to see the apartment, I've got enough to write a screwball comedy.

—Don't forget the pain and loneliness, that's my strong suit.

—No, no. It'll be a dramatic comedy. I'll get writing.

And I did. After three months I had the first draft of *Are You Seriously Asking Me If I'm Alright?!*, we had trouble getting financing. I was a newcomer, as was León. We might have been well-known in theater, but nobody was sure that we would work in the cinema. And people were suspicious that we wanted to make a screwball comedy. We were known for the opposite.

The filming of *Are You Seriously Asking Me* went well, except for León's violent jealousy of the rest of the cast. There were two young actresses who proved to have riotous comic skills that drove León crazy because they were stealing every scene. Pure jealousy. He said he would never do an ensemble comedy again. He wasn't funny, but he didn't need to be. Every plot thread led to him, and the comedy came from how he dealt with them naturally and confidently. That funny side of his character emerged in these screwball situations that left him no time to think about the fact he had been dumped. I was happy, although every night I had to put up with his ridiculous complaints.

Once the editing was finished, the only thing left was to create the music, but we didn't have the money to commission an original score or license songs and music that we loved. León thought this was a minor hiccup, but I had to be very firm: in cinema, the music copyright is sacred. If you don't pay, they can have the film taken off the screen. Just like that. León didn't understand, but he knew that I was serious.

There was one possibility worth exploring: the communist Eastern European countries did not pay music royalties or copyright if a movie premiered in their territories. In return, a creator using music from those countries did not have to pay royalties or performing rights fees. So I started to look for music for the film on records recorded in communist countries. And I found some real gems: a Stravinsky tango, Shostakovich, Cuban *filin*, Bola de Nieve, Béla Bartók, performed by magnificent national orchestras. I have very eclectic tastes, and the mix of all these artists gave the narrative a structure that was simultaneously solid and light.

The film was released, and in all honesty, it was a huge success. No one could tell that the principal character got on terribly with his female costars throughout filming. The freshness, the rhythm, and a very inspired script took the world by storm.

Despite the success, León vowed never to make another ensemble comedy.

—I wish they could all be out like this —I said—. I wish all our films could reach an audience of three million in Spain and get distribution in twenty countries. What's the problem?

The problem was it was not León who shone brightest in the film. He was "good," but to him, good was an insult. To avoid making a queer movie, he had insisted on surrounding himself with actresses, with the result that the actresses had eaten him alive.

León swore he would never make another movie.

The Streetcar and the Night

Years later, we went to the Filmoteca to see *Opening Night*, a film by John Cassavetes that had never been theatrically released in Spain.

I was surprised that León decided to come with me. He didn't like Cassavetes, but I was passionate about his work. He was the American independent filmmaker who had most influenced me, even if León didn't quite see how. *A Woman Under the Influence*, *Faces*, *Shadows* had bored him to tears, he preferred Hollywood and its trickery.

Opening Night stars Gena Rowlands, ably supported by Ben Gazzara, a tough guy whose eyes seem to harbor a sardonic smile. Over time, the director played by Gazzara in the film would become the director role (film or theater) with which I most identified.

The film tells the story of a theater company doing out-of-town previews in various states before opening in New York, while dealing with a leading lady who, besides being an alcoholic, is going insane. For León and me, the film was a revelation, and our shared enthusiasm and the fact that we were vibrating in unison brought us together again.

We left the cinema singing its praises and making wild gesticulations, like characters in a Woody Allen picture. It's amazing when a film grabs you like that and when the person with you is even more excited than you are.

Before we got home, León neatly summed up the mark it had made on us:

—It's about time we made our second movie.

—I thought you said you'd never make another movie.

—When I said that, I hadn't seen *Opening Night*—León said.

I looked at him in amazement, I knew all too well the tone in which he had said that, his unshakable determination.

León spent the next few days making notes. We went to every screening at the Filmoteca so we would know the movie by heart. (Later we got the DVD, but when León is inspired by a work and decides to really get into it, he doesn't give it much thought. He digests it, makes it his own, forgets the original, and communicates his enthusiasm to me so I can give it form and words.)

This was his plan. We'd make a film about a theater company touring the provinces with our second version of *A Streetcar Named Desire*, starring Blanco del Bosque.

—*Streetcar* again? —I said—. We've already done it twice in the theater.

—It doesn't matter what play the company is doing —León said—. What's important is the hell that the actor playing Blanco (me) has to go through with the rest of the cast and the play.

—So you want to play Myrtle? Gena Rowlands?

—I know a thing or two about drinking, to say nothing about fighting with directors and writers. This way you can channel all the things you hate about me but never dared put on paper. I'll fuck the actor who plays Kowalski (who has to be played by a young, muscular careerist, who's not gay), and I'm no stranger to Myrtle's madness. Like her, I'm a star. I know the boredom of the fans waiting for autographs outside the theater door on a rainy night when you've had it up to here. I've got it all, and I've got you to write and direct me. It's a character in her autumn years, Myrtle has problems with her age. Daniel, I'm not a kid anymore, I have to choose roles that fit my age.

—Don't we have to clear the rights? —I said—. Gena Rowlands is still alive . . .

—We'll pitch it as an homage. We'll put her name in the closing credits.

—An homage, that's an excuse used by plagiarists and rip-off artists.

—You'll make sure our case is different. You always do. I'm not Gena Rowlands, but I know what it's like to tour and have problems with the company, and you know it too . . . The world of *Opening Night* is our world.

—But they could tour with a different play . . .

—No. Our second *Streetcar* is perfect. The Blanco del Bosque character neatly dovetails with Myrtle (we'd have to call him Mirto), they complement each other. What's important is that the crisis of an actor coming to terms with getting older forces him to stage an almost unworkable version of *Streetcar*. (Remember the problems you had adapting the play to suit me, and we already *know* that it works, and all of your reservations will work perfectly for the director of this *Streetcar*.) He's constantly challenging the writer and the director, you can use yourself as a model. Now, I realize that there's nothing larger-than-life about our *Opening Night*. On the contrary, it's utterly naturalistic. It flows naturally. The characters live in constant tension, but this pressure cooker explodes when, as she leaves the theater, Myrtle's car runs over a young fan and kills her. This is the final straw for Myrtle/Mirto. For fuck's sake, I'm giving you everything here, I'll have my name on the screenplay too.

And he got what he wanted. He added:

—I know you'll create an amazing character for the director, you've got loads of autobiographical material. But I'll make sure that Myrtle shines. In her descent into hell she needs to take the audience with her, the way Gena Rowlands took us.

He had me almost convinced. I didn't want to tell him, but it was true that the twin subversions, of *Streetcar* and of *Opening Night*, dovetailed perfectly. My job was to adapt the character of Myrtle for León, *Streetcar* was his already. And it's true that our lives, his as an actor and mine as a writer/director, gave me rich material on which to draw so I could give flesh and authenticity to the director played by Ben Gazzara, and his crazed, drunken star, devastatingly portrayed by Gena Rowlands.

—You'd have to be as magnificent as Gena Rowlands and

I'd have to be as brilliant as Cassavetes *and* Joan Blondell, the actress who plays the writer —I said just for something to say. It was obvious that he'd already persuaded me.

—No one in Spain has even heard of them. Nobody will make comparisons, ours will be the original. A lot of critics will see it as confessional.

—May I remind you I've only ever directed one film?

—And it was a huge success, though I still don't understand why. This time we'll do an edgy drama. It's what we've always done in theater, it's our specialty.

This is an excellent example of León appropriating things that were not his. Not only was he prepared to rip off Cassavetes's work, but he was suggesting I build the character of the director around the doubts and reservations I had about gender-swapping Blanche DuBois, and in doing so, become the victim of the tortures he had inflicted on me when I tried to subvert Tennessee Williams's work. He was a master of misappropriation. At times I was spellbound by his talent, and on those occasions, despite all my reservations and attempts at sanity, I would end up swept away by León's wildly eccentric and disrespectful concepts. I'd never have dared do such things on my own because my respect for the original turned into prejudice.

I wrote *The Streetcar and the Night*. We shot it. It was an international success. León won lots of awards. The film was nominated at the Oscars and the Golden Globes. I had to acknowledge the chemistry between León and me, even if our relationship would barely survive, or only when he managed to drag me to a point where the embarrassment I should have felt at the plagiarism he was suggesting set my imagination on fire. A fire that burned me in every sense, though he always came through it unscathed.

León had started to lose his memory, on the film set there were crib sheets everywhere. Ever since he found out that Brando filled his set with crib sheets, he decided it was time to let his memory take a break. At first, I was surprised that he was so insistent about the character's age, he hadn't yet turned fifty.

With *The Streetcar and the Night*, León rekindled the fire of inspiration in me. But for a long time we had been living through a very destructive period. This was not a relationship breaking up, it was being utterly demolished, disaster was looming. And I no longer had the reserves to fight. And no desire to do so. I knew that our time had come to its end, in every sense. Appearances seemed to contradict me. We still worked brilliantly together, but I had lost faith in us. León, on the other hand, had not lost one iota of confidence in us both. He had just recently become aware that physically he looked older than he was. And in his line of work, physical appearance and memory are crucial. For a man with no memory, the cinema is easier than the theater, which is why he wanted *The Streetcar and the Night* to be a film.

SO HERE WE ARE, in a hospital, a year after the impossible combination of the second *Streetcar* and our theft of Cassavetes's

43

masterpiece. A few hours earlier I had surgery for kidney stones. I slept all afternoon. At night I was more alert and sometimes complained about the catheter. León said it must be *interesting* (*Interesting?* I thought) to have a catheter where I had it, in my penis, an appendage that had given me and many others so much pleasure. (*Others?* I thought silently. My penis, like everything else I possessed, had been devoted exclusively to him, to León.)

A minute later I heard him snoring. I would have liked to sleep, but I couldn't drift off with all that snoring. A fly flapping its wings can wake me up. I'm a light sleeper. I always travel with wax earplugs, because there are thousands of mysterious noises (especially in hotels) that lurk in the darkness only to reveal themselves the moment you decide to go to sleep. A hospital is a kind of hotel where the guests are ill and there are lots of noises. The little box of wax plugs was at the bottom of my rucksack, in the closet of my hospital room. I couldn't move. And I didn't dare wake León to get them for me.

This sums up my romantic and professional relationship with him in a nutshell. He would steal my words and make them his own. His creative process consisted of firing my imagination with any banal or unusual allusion, and once my imagination developed the idea, however whimsical, he was there, waiting to pluck the fruit, make it his own, and let me take charge of the staging. Of course, on a romantic level there had been no, or very few months of, faithfulness.

My ideas, my life, however much León shared them, did

not all belong to him. When I say that he exploited me, I'm not referring to the plays or the films we made together, or not only to them. And I'm not complaining. Obviously, it was hurtful in the beginning, but I got used to it. I accepted (not his fault, but mine) that I simply had to deal with his eating disorders, his drug problems, his sexual hang-ups. I existed only as a means for him to fulfill his artistic fantasies. I'm not saying that's nothing. For years he kept me in a whirlwind of excitement, kept me exploring and discovering new territory. My relationship with León, who could be unfaithful, even cruel, wasn't all sacrifice. I was also enriched by it, and that was the best education I could have had. But that was a long time ago.

THE MIRROR
CEREMONY

The black carriage transporting the Count cleaves the night, leaving greater darkness in its wake. This is a treacherous route for man and beast alike. The carriage jolts along a dirt track, marked out by an overhead pulley that serves as a lifeline between the peak of Mount Athos and the village it depends on for its basic needs. On the summit, remote, shielded, isolated, stands the monastery of a cloistered order of monks. The carriage comes to a halt outside the gates. The Count telepathically communicates with the beasts that draw his carriage. It is pitch-dark. Black on inky black. The gleam in his eyes, and those of his horses, helps him find the monastery door. Darkness has never been a problem for the Count.

Before knocking, he bids farewell to carriage and horses,

embraces the carriage and kisses the horses' thick lips. The animals let out a whinny that pierces the walls of the monastery like a lightning bolt.

The Count turns his back on the emotional scene, not wishing to watch his hitherto inseparable companions disappear.

He strikes the door of the monastery with his fist and waits a few minutes. He is greeted by Brother Anselmo, the watchman who, in his younger years, wished to be an alchemist until Almighty God, or rather one of His earthly messengers, dissuaded him. And so Anselmo joined the community on Mount Athos, where, when not absorbed in prayer, he devoted his time to tending the garden that, in time, became a veritable kitchen garden that fed the entire congregation. Anselmo and his savior and soul mate, Brother Hortensio, have been given special dispensation to spend whatever time that nature demands cultivating the garden. There are also hens, and therefore eggs and chicks.

Drowsy and puzzled, the monk stares at the Count.

—What brings you here, señor?

—Please excuse my inopportune arrival, Father, but I come a great distance and could not know at what time I would arrive.

The visitor's appearance and noble bearing do not go unnoticed by the monk. From somewhere deep inside, Brother Hortensio appears, having heard the knocking at the door. He watches as Brother Anselmo echoes his question to the curious visitor.

—What can I do for you, señor?

—I have decided to retreat from the world and devote my life to prayer. I would like to speak to the rector.

—I shall try to alert the rector, Brother Benito, but I cannot promise anything.

The Count steps through the austere doorway and waits. Brother Hortensio approaches Brother Anselmo and whispers:

—Who is this man? What does he want?

—I don't know, he is asking to see the rector.

—Tell him to come another day. This is not the hour to be troubling Brother Benito.

—He has decided to withdraw from the world.

—Here? I do not like the look of him, I think there has been some misunderstanding. Perhaps someone has played a cruel joke on him.

—Nevertheless, I must inform the rector.

The Count waits, silent and ramrod straight, while the two monks hold their brief conclave. He stares at Brother Anselmo, then at Brother Hortensio, neither of whom can hold his gaze for more than a second, a gaze that is shimmering and opaque, heavy as metal. The gaze of a creature who, though appearing to be humble, radiates an intimidating superiority.

—Is there some problem? —inquires the Count.

—No problem, I will go to the rector now and see if he is awake.

Brother Hortensio stays with the Count.

—Do not look at me as though I am a threat —the Count says, simultaneously imploring and commanding.

It is ever thus with him, this talent to provoke an emotion and its opposite.

—Are you quite sure of that? —says the monk.

—I have never thought of myself in such terms. Perhaps there was a time when I was dangerous . . .

—What do you know of the life we lead up here?

—I have heard much about this monastery —the Count says—, but, please, instruct me, you who live here.

—Ours is a life of abstinence and sacrifice. Of devotion to prayer. We do only such work as is necessary to our survival. The rest is silence, hunger, and contemplation. Brother Anselmo, who boasts a knowledge of chemistry, works to distill remedies from the medicinal plants I grow in the garden. Over time, we created a natural laboratory. But I cannot promise that we can save you should you fall ill. Ours is a savage and secluded life.

—I am disposed to accept such conditions.

—You will not be permitted to receive visitors. Your roots and your past have no place in this monastery.

—I have long since forgotten the world, and it, in turn, has forgotten me. Your words merely confirm that I made no mistake in coming here.

They are interrupted by Anselmo, who cannot conceal his nervousness.

—The rector has agreed to see you. He is waiting in his cell.

Brother Hortensio contemplates his companion's unease. The presence of the Count has made an impression on them both, and he is not sure that this is a good sign.

Brother Anselmo leads the Count into a room as spartan as the hall.

The Count has studied the life of the monastery and that of its rector, who is lauded for his self-cruelty and disregard for his own biological needs. Sanctity was the only explanation one could give to such a self-destructive nature.

While religion invariably strips life of its more pleasurable aspects, Brother Benito tested the limits of human endurance, reducing his life to a perpetual penance. His daily routine defied the very exigencies of his human nature. His survival was living proof that miracles were possible.

The cell is empty, the floor is flagstone, the only furnishings are a wooden table, a chair, and a bed. The Count looks through the bed (to him, there are no walls, no bedsteads, his gaze is boundless and all-seeing) and sees the rector lying on the hard stone beneath. But the Count has wearied even of this skill and does not flaunt it. He hopes the monastery will expunge his many powers and reduce them to one.

As for Brother Benito, he would like to know what the newcomer is thinking, what he looks like. He tries to look through the bed as well, to see the Count as clearly as he is himself seen, but in vain. He can see only his shoes and ankles. The rector emerges from beneath the bed and greets the newcomer. They exchange a look that is more akin to an arm-wrestling contest than two men simply looking at one another. In this contest, neither wins. The Count adopts his humblest demeanor and withdraws his burning gaze from the rector. He is keenly aware of the effect of his presence and struggles to contain it. He strives to appear less than he is.

The monk's gaunt face betrays a will of iron, self-confidence, and a deep mistrust of others. His eyes are beautiful and, despite their apparent harshness, shine with the mysterious translucence seen in sacred icons. Of all the emotions he harbors about himself and about life, a single one predominates: dissatisfaction. His eyes express the torment of a man who cannot quite accept the gulf that separates dreams from reality.

The great renown of the monk and of his writings had reached the Count's ears, but the rector is unaware of the identity of his majestic visitor. His initial impression is excellent. He is struck by the combination of opulence and pallor, brilliance and exhaustion, and the figure of the Count radiates something undeniably mystical. He is at once awe-inspiring and hollow. Never before has the monk been so mesmerized by anyone. He understands the nervousness with which Brother Anselmo announced his arrival.

—I am a count from Transylvania, and I have come a great distance so that I might make retreat in your monastery.

—Do you know the rules that govern life within these walls?

—Silence, solitude, hunger, and contemplation. I wish to

withdraw from the world and live solely in sanctity and in contemplation of Christ Jesus.

—Allow me to insist. Do you understand what it means to renounce the worldly pleasures and comforts to which you have ready access? A single glance tells me you are accustomed to a life of ease. Could it be that you are only momentarily jaded or disillusioned? I have known such cases.

—It is not so with me. I have tasted of everything, but the world, its pleasures and its ideas, no longer excites or interests me. For years I have lived a solitary temperate existence, surrounded by animals. I travel constantly, and so have no attachment to anything or any person.

The monk feels drawn to this stranger, in his totality.

I knew that one day he would knock on our door, the monk thinks. *A short while ago, this very night, my slumber was pierced by a lightning bolt that heralded his coming. I sensed him before I met him.* And the Count, reading his thoughts, knows that it was no flash of lightning but the neighing of his horses that heralded his coming, but he says nothing because he senses that Brother Benito prefers to believe that he has otherworldly powers and delights in flaunting them.

Mentally, silently, the two men converse with their eyes. The monk cannot make out what the Count is thinking. He cannot think what else to say to him, so he simply states the obvious:

—It is too late, or too early. I shall have Brother Anselmo show you to your cell. The first few months will be a trial. If your intentions are sincere, you will find a home here. Perhaps you could work with Brother Hortensio in the garden, if he has need of you. But there is not much to do. Your soul will find ample time for prayer and meditation. Tomorrow, I leave to make a journey. When I return, you shall let me know whether your wishes have changed. I hope to find you still here.

—I shall be. Do not doubt it.

Brother Benito is periodically absent from the convent. He has read Matthew G. Lewis's novel *The Monk* and dreams of being confronted by the temptations that lure the novel's protagonist to his perdition but has had no such good fortune . . . although the presence of the Count may change this mediocre fate. Although he would never confess as much, he likes to travel, to break the tedious monotony of the monastery. On his journeys, he revels in his status as a living saint, a guide to the most important souls in the country and a prestigious counselor to important people. A cruel seducer of misguided men and women. But, for all his dealings with the rich and powerful, not once has he come face-to-face with an evil against which to pit his faith and triumph, to be the living saint that people say he is.

Strangely, the journey that follows the Count's visit is fruitless, both for Brother Benito and for his followers. The monk is distracted, he is no longer thinking about Lewis's *The Monk*, he cannot get the Count out of his mind. And he finds this thought deeply distressing. As a penance, he prolongs the journey, thus keeping his burning desire to return to the monastery at bay. Perhaps the devil has chosen this extraordinary Count to tempt him. And he finds some solace in the fear this thought stirs in him.

AS THE RECTOR promised, the Count is exempt from all domestic duties. When the bell tolls, he joins his companions in the refectory and in the church, only to disappear again. And, though they watch him, none dares disturb him. Brother Benito left word that they should ignore him. He wanted the Count to know indifference and insignificance.

Over time, the Count begins to absent himself from the refectory and, at some point, stops going altogether. He scarcely eats. The brothers' vow of discretion coupled with the rector's counsel prevent them from inquiring about his health. Brother Anselmo fears this discretion might prove fatal for the Count. Brother Hortensio, being jealous, hopes it is.

After some weeks, the rector returns. Never has he been so eager to come back to the monastery. He is quick to inquire after his guest.

Wonder, astonishment, envy, and bewilderment sum up the general impression. The Count's days, he is told, are divided between the chapel and his cell. He rarely wanders in the garden, and never pauses to gaze at the sun. The twilights and the dawns, whose ineffable beauty would justify the existence of the monastery and its residents, hold no appeal for him. It has been weeks since he last set foot in the refectory and no one has surprised him picking potatoes, onions, or lettuce in the kitchen garden. The two monks whose cells adjoin the Count's attest that they have heard him get up in the night to go to chapel. On many early mornings, they have found him, before the altar, in ecstasy. He did not seem human, his hieratic figure was hard as stone and dark as blackest night.

The community concedes that the newcomer's conduct is beyond reproach. However, the prevailing atmosphere is one of worry and unease.

—I thought as much —the rector says—. It is why I tarried so long in returning.

Nobody understands his words, but Brother Benito enjoys unsettling the monks with absurd phrases that even he does not understand.

After a moment spent collecting his thoughts, the rector approaches the Count's cell, troubled by his guest's lack of curiosity. He finds the door locked, but has a master key that opens every door. The cell is empty, the window sealed tight. The only light comes from two small slits in the wooden window frame.

The bed is unrumpled. There is no trace of a body. The rector turns to leave, but before he can, he is stopped in his tracks by the Count's voice.

—How was your journey?

The rector starts and turns around. His guest nimbly crawls from beneath the bed. It had not occurred to him to look under the bed, believing that he alone slept on the bare flagstones. With a quiver of complicity, he asks:

—What are you doing under the bed?

—Resting. I prefer the floor.

—As do I.

The coolness of the stone floor has chilled the Count's face, it is impossible to detect the slightest emotion. The rector's mental powers are famous, or so he claims, and the others are generally prepared to humor him, but when he is with the Count, everything is different. In the presence of the Count, he feels transparent, naked, light as a feather.

He is disturbed by this new sensation. Confused and lacking inspiration, he silently leaves.

The Count knows that, ever since the rector arrived, he has been watching the Count. All the brothers do so, but the rector, given his status and power, makes no attempt to hide the fact. In order not to arouse suspicion, the Count forgoes his nightly visits to the chapel for a time. And he adds a little charade: every morning before dawn, he goes down to the kitchen garden to stock up on food, which he later throws away. Before these outings, he smears his face and hands with a thick cream he brought with him.

On the sixth night, he feels a pressing need to kneel before God in the solitude of night. Before visiting the chapel, he ensures that the brothers are asleep or in their cells. Soundlessly, the Count moves through the corridors as though he does not touch the ground, but hovers over it, and through the doors, he hears only snoring.

When he arrives at Brother Benito's cell, he hears not snoring but whip-strokes and whimpers. He stands motionless before the door and sees that there is no key. The vacant lock invites his gaze, perhaps deliberately. The Count accepts the invitation, kneels and looks. He watches the monk violently lashing his bare back until the floor is spattered with blood. It is an edifying sight, one that suggests new avenues of communication between the two men. The Count thinks about this for a moment, then decides to give free rein to his piety as he had planned, in his natural home, the chapel.

He enters the chapel and prostrates himself before a vast crucifix that looms over one of the altars. He remains in this posture for a time, still as stone, deep in prayer. Then he raises his head, his eyes glowing like the embers of a guttering bonfire.

He is not alone in the chapel. Brother Benito has followed him and is watching from his cloak of shadows.

The Count approaches the unnaturally large crucifix. The carved wooden Christ begins to gush blood from every wound. First the feet, then the chest, the hands, the corners of the mouth, the temples. The Count rises into the air and presses his frantic mouth to each and every wellspring. Not a single drop is spilled on the ground. An awestruck Brother Benito contemplates the miracle. Before his very eyes, the mysteries of the Eucharist are revealed in all their magnitude.

Having licked every inch of the carved wood, the body

of the Count has shrunk to the size of that of a black bird (a swallow, thinks the rector). Had he been closer, he would have seen it was a bat.

The bird perches on the head of Christ and diligently pecks at the droplets of blood that still maculate the crown of thorns. Then, resuming his human form, the Count prostrates himself before the image of the cross, rigid with devotion.

Brother Benito feels himself gripped by that same intense devotion, but it is provoked not by Christ, but the Count, whose lips still retain traces of divine blood. The Count brings a hand to his mouth, attempting to hide the blood. He has sensed the presence of the monk and his fevered desire to lick the Count's bloody lips. The realization of the monk's desire scalds the Count's mouth.

Brother Benito knows he has been unmasked. The contempt he sees in the Count's eyes hurts much more than the lashes of his whip.

He leaves the chapel and spends the rest of the night trembling with confusion in his cell.

In a state of great agitation, Brother Benito does not leave his cell all day. He answers to no one. In an obsessive, childish tantrum, he pledges not to open the door unless it is the Count who knocks.

The following day, Brother Anselmo is so insistent that the rector has no choice but to open the door. The disciple brings food and homemade tinctures for his cold, the whole monastery heard him coughing during the night. The rector refuses everything and asks how long it has been since anyone saw the Count eat.

—More than a month, I think.

—If he can do it, I can.

Brother Anselmo gently protests. The rector reproaches him:

—You should practice greater tact and more indifference.

—I worry about you.

TWO WEEKS LATER, Brother Anselmo concedes defeat and knocks on the door of the Count's cell.

—The rector is ill and wishes to see you.

The Count had not missed the rector, because he thought him abroad on one of his journeys and, truth be told, because he had not thought of him at all.

The rector's cell is a poor simulacrum of his own. Not only does the rector sleep on the floor beneath the bed, but the night table, the crude wardrobe, and a crucifix have the same placement as in the Count's cell.

As soon as they are alone, the conversation is swift and pointed.

—What ails you, Brother Benito?

—My strength has abandoned me.

—Try to eat something.

—I shall eat what you eat.

—When did I become an exemplar?

—"The virtuous soul that is alone and without a master is

like a long lone burning coal. It will grow colder rather than hotter." Teach me to receive communion!

—Fasting makes you delirious.

—And it makes you lie. Since you showed me true communion, the other no longer serves me.

—What you are saying is absurd and ludicrous, not to mention sinful, in your own parlance.

—And I say that unless you reveal your secret to me, I will not allow you to stay in this monastery a moment longer.

The Count reflects for a moment.

—Very well.

—Do not leave me, Count!

—What is it you want?

—I beg of you!

—Very well. Calm yourself and listen to the story I tell.

My story: I am a vampire. Literature and idle minds have fashioned many legends about my kind. This is no justification, still less a vindication. I have no interest in vampirizing anyone. I am like your mystics. I like to be alone, left to follow my own devices and desires.

But I was not always so. I, too, have known long periods of turmoil and mild intemperance.

Vampires are a curious species, I do not deny it. We are endowed with fewer powers than man supposes, and fewer weaknesses than we imagine. Nothing but fairy tales and fears, dammit! Of all the things that are said of us, but one is true: we cast no reflection in mirrors nor in the eyes of others nor on the surface of still water. We are reflected only in the fantasies of others, like the one you are experiencing now. In dreams, our shadows lengthen, and our day is night.

The rector looks at him, enthralled.

There is no greater solitude than to know that you are not accompanied by your own image. The testament of others, even that of loved ones, is not enough. Being unable to see my face, I came to believe I had no face at all. I was convinced that, if God existed, He belonged to the family of mirrors and, for some reason I did not understand, chose to deny our existence.

The constant proselytizing of my fellow creatures stems more from vengeance than from bloodlust, more from rage than from the need to sate our thirst. Each new victim that surrenders to our fangs is a victory before the Mirror-God, an image that we snatch from him forever.

By extension of our hatred of the mirror, we hate the Sign of the Cross. It is an irrational cliché that vampires have not yet overcome. We equate the cross with God Himself, but they are nothing alike. I have never seen God, yet over every altar I can see a cross. This monastery is filled with crosses, and they do not trouble me. They comfort me.

In my existence as a vampire, as I have said, I have endured great crises. Like others, I disowned and vilified my nature. I could not bear the incessant languor in which I lived, the orgies no longer entertained me. Yet, blood was still vital. For many years I was a nihilist. I hunted only when I had no choice. I gave up human throats and I fed on any source of animal blood, even the most impure: chickens, rabbits, dogs, even my own horses.

It was one of my horses that unexpectedly showed me the way.

At that time, I spent my nights inside my coffin, reading by the light of my eyes. I was fascinated by Jainism, Buddhism, and Christian mysticism. Have I not seen you read *Dark Night of the Soul*? I read everything I could lay my hands on.

I became convinced that, if I wanted to end this melancholy, I would have to take the risk.

I began by visiting monasteries of architectural note. My gaze is deep, and from afar I peered into the interior of the chapels without daring to enter. Like a child about to jump from a diving board for the first time, I took a long time to make up my mind.

It happened on one such excursion. I was lying on the grass in the moonlight, near the church of El Salvador del Mundo, on the outskirts of a village in La Mancha. I was surprised to find it open, and could scarce believe my eyes when I saw my horse meekly circling inside, given that the animal is also a vampire. It was I who bit him. I who made him so.

The time had come to gather momentum and jump.

And so I did, I went inside.

The church was empty. The high altar was dominated by an image of the Savior of the world. A crucifix as vast as my curiosity dominated the space. I approached the altar, still looking at Christ, and knelt before him. I was not swallowed by an earthquake, I did not see the heavens rent asunder to reveal their contents, nor was I struck by lightning and set ablaze. The night was still and calm. It was the first time I had seen that image, and the very sight of it brought me a new and utter peace.

Suddenly, something extraordinary happened. From his every wound, his feet, his knees, his chest, his mouth, his palms, his temples, this Christ began to spurt blood. However small it was, each wound painted on the carved wood became a sudden, irrepressible source of life. Paralyzed, I watched the miracle. It was then I heard Him speak to me:

—I am the one, the only source of life. Whomsoever drinks of my blood shall need no other nourishment. —I heard it, like an echo, deep inside me.

He needed no more words, and nor did I. I approached the crucifix and drank the liquid that for a long time flowed from his wounds. With my lips, I lapped up the pool of blood that had formed on the floor. And I flew like an airplane on the day it was first invented.

I returned to the castle, eager to tell my companions of

the marvel I had discovered. But none believed me. On the contrary, no sooner had I finished my story, than they looked at me with contempt. I offered to provide a demonstration, but to no avail. They had no wish to change. Routine afforded them security, and they believed that abstinence had driven me insane.

I fled the castle, leaving everything behind. I traveled to many places in Spain. I met one of your acolytes, who showed me your letters, and I instantly recognized myself in them. I came here for the purposes you already know. If I have not spoken before now, it was not out of cruelty. Being rejected by my fellow vampires showed me that individual solutions do not save others. And vampirism is a road of no return, one I would not advise to anyone.

Brother Benito says four words:
—Make me a vampire.
Faced with the rector's unwavering determination, the Count underscores the torments of his kind. He speaks of the pain of being unable to see oneself, the opacity of mirrors and all reflecting surfaces that depend on the light. The rector considers these a small price in return for what he will receive. Garlic is merely a foolish legend. And sunlight, though it bothers the Count, is bearable; he has sensitive skin that needs a solid layer of moisturizer to protect him.

In the face of the rector's single-mindedness, the Count

has no choice but to make the necessary arrangements for the new ordination.

BROTHER BENITO IS as nervous as a bride. And the Count no longer thinks it is such a bad idea to make him a vampire. He has begun to enjoy the idea of not being alone.

They broach the subject of eternity and death. The Count confides that should the rector wish to leave the world, he need only drive a stake into his heart. For this he would need the help of someone else. It would not do to do it alone.

The rector does not even want to discuss the subject.

—I do not envy the saints their bliss of the afterlife.

—You are right, vampirism itself is a different life.

In keeping with its magnitude, the ceremony will be simple and intimate.

The night before the ceremony, someone claims to see a large mirror flying through the sky near the village closest to the monastery. A lady from a local hamlet reports its disappearance, but however much she is questioned, she cannot say how or what happened except that her mirror vanished. Only the rector and the Count know the truth. Taking the form of a bat, the Count took the mirror from her bedroom in his jaws and carried it to the convent.

They set up the huge mirror next to the altar of the unnaturally large, eternally suffering Christ. Nothing more is needed. Everything is in readiness.

With great delicacy, the Count solemnizes the ordination.

—Look closely at your face. Nose, eyes, lips, cheeks, eyebrows, chin, hair, ears. Open your mouth and look inside. Do not forget your tongue . . . stick it out and look at it, because you will not see it again. Remove your clothes, garment by garment, make no haste. Now look closely in the mirror at each limb. Revel in it. Who would have thought that you had such a handsome, sinewy body?

The rector obeys the words of the Count, until he is completely naked.

Modesty has meant he cannot remember seeing himself naked since he was a boy. He feels an unexpected nostalgia. He strokes his legs, his chest, his shoulders, his arms, his penis . . . Indeed, he is more handsome than he could have imagined.

—I like my body.

—You still have time to turn back, to enjoy it for a while.

—That time is passed.

For a few moments, the rector continues to exult. He strikes different poses and admires his body from different angles.

—I am ready —he says.

The Count approaches and embraces him. In the mirror, the monk sees only his own reflection. His muscles tense, his arms wrap around the vampire's chest, although the mirror does not reflect it. Never losing sight of his own face, the monk surrenders to the Count. He arches his back in a gesture of rapture. In that instant, the Count's fangs pierce his neck. The rector's image in the mirror vanishes, and he falls to the ground.

The vampire pounces on him, draining his arteries with savage frenzy.

They lie, sprawled on top of one other, as if they had just made passionate love.

When the rector comes to himself, he looks at the crucifix above the altar.

The Count helps him to his feet. Blood begins to flow from the wounds of the Christ. The couple hurl themselves upon the carved wood and feed upon the nourishing blood with wild abandon.

After this banquet, transformed into bats, they flutter from the chapel and lose themselves in the dark of a night that now holds no mysteries.

THIS NOCTURNAL, NUPTIAL flight and the ceremony of the mirror become a new initiation rite for the mystic-vampiric order born of the union of Brother Benito and the Count.

They try to forget the world, and to have the world forget them. Many generations of farmers living in a nearby village are struck by the curious longevity of the monks. But superstition and fear create walls that are stronger and more impregnable than the curiosity of men.

As the Count told Brother Benito, vampires and mystics were destined to find common ground.

JOANNA, THE BEAUTIFUL MADWOMAN

In the Alcázar de Segovia was a room that, together with the chapel and her private quarters, numbered among those favored by the Catholic queen: the sewing room. When her royal duties permitted, the queen would spend whole afternoons here, sewing with her daughters. Nothing pleased her more. Isabella was as fine a queen as she was a wife and mother. For her, an exemplary Catholic, one was as important as the other.

—Before she may govern a country, a woman must first learn to govern her household —she often admonished her daughters, Isabella, Catherine, and Joanna.

The last of these had little inclination for the duties her

august mother attempted to inculcate in her, and sometimes, as on this occasion, dared show it:

—But what does the kingdom stand to gain from any of us learning how to sew?

—Heed me, child. My husband, your father, has never worn a shirt whose threads I did not weave myself.

—But in Spain we have magnificent weavers for this very task —Joanna challenged again.

—True, but my noble husband would not have worn them in the same way. Moreover, had we entrusted the work to another woman, we should have had to pay her, and when you are grown, Joanna dear, you will realize that the needs of our people are many, and that whatever we save, it will never be enough.

Doña Joanna said no more. Reluctantly, she carried on the work, adding her silence to that of her sisters. But this apparent tranquility was short-lived, broken by an unexpected howl. It was once again Doña Joanna who caught the queen's attention.

—What is the matter, child?

—I pricked myself —wailed the tearful Infanta.

The queen chided her:

—A fitting punishment for your inattentiveness. In the future be more careful in what you do.

But the Infanta did not seem to hear. Her mouth fell open and she turned from the work. The Catholic queen was astounded by this indiscipline.

—Mother, I am dead with sleep —said Joanna, dragging out the words as though something were preventing her from enunciating.

—You were wide awake a moment since. What can this mean?

—I do not know. Suddenly, I am exceedingly wea . . .

Before she could finish the sentence, the Infanta was sound asleep. She was carried to her bed where, to the consternation of the royal family, days passed and Joanna did not wake up. And they knew not what to do.

This mysterious malady distressed the king and queen. Isabella, as was her wont, dedicated her grief to Christ Crucified and sought comfort in Him as her chief ally. To this end she ordered masses and novenas throughout the country. She wanted the whole kingdom, especially those noble families so intimately acquainted with splendor and dissipation, to join in her torment and make sacrifice with her. After many weeks of popular piety, still the Crucified Christ did not take pity on the sleeping Infanta. Queen Isabella, who did not shrink from any sacrifice, decided to mortify her flesh (it was not the first time she had done so) so that she might better merit divine intervention. Her husband, King Ferdinand, suggested other means, but she, who behind closed doors despised her husband, scornfully rebuked him:

—If you are too fainthearted, leave it to me. I will mortify my flesh for both of us, and do so in your presence so that, in seeing me suffer, you too may suffer a little, and so have something to offer Him who died upon the cross for all mankind.

The sight of the queen's self-flagellation was repellent to her noble husband. He confessed as much to his spiritual advisor:

—The queen is insensitive to pain. She orders that the floors of the halls be strewn with burning embers and shards of glass, and calmly walks over them as across a soft carpet. She has always relished the cruelest mortifications, but never before has she gone to such extremes. For several years, she slept on a huge stone, but lately she has had a bed of daggers made, upon whose sharp points she lies each night like a fakir. She never complains, but I find the spectacle unbearable.

After many days of fruitless waiting, the royal staff, aware of the Infanta's illness, were consumed with doubt, but still the queen refused to give up. She continued to submit to gruesome tortures in the sight of God, for there was always a crucifix into which Isabella gazed as into a mirror, and of the king.

Four months of constant sleep passed, and Isabella threatened to have herself crucified if Joanna did not wake. It was an increasingly difficult state of affairs. The royal couple did not wish the populace to learn the truth and made every effort to appear normal, but despite their secrecy, rumors had already begun to circulate that the king and queen were holding the Infanta Joanna hostage.

Isabella persisted in her escalating mortification. She commanded that a cross three meters in height be erected on one of the towers of the Alcázar so that all could see it, and was on the threshold of having herself crucified when she was succored by a deep and radiant voice that could be none other than the voice of God.

—Isabella, forsake this mortification and fret not about your troubles. It is not in the bosom of grief, but in the midst of pleasures and feasts, that you will find the key that awakens your daughter.

The queen did not doubt that the voice was genuine, but she was disconcerted by the divine words. Pleasures? Feasts? What kind of pleasures? What kind of feasts? Religious feasts?

—No —once more she heard the booming voice of God—, secular, boisterous, traditional, violent feasts.

The queen despised pleasures and feasts, but the deep, radiant voice left no room for doubt. It was utterly precise. Only in pleasure and amusements of every kind save religious would she find the key to bring an end to Joanna's mysterious slumber.

To the jubilant astonishment of the noblemen, Isabella decreed an end to the strict mourning commanded after the death of her son Fernando some months earlier, and in its place she announced a return to dissipation, extravagance, and gaiety.

When Ferdinand asked the reason for this change of heart, the queen cryptically replied:

—God works in mysterious ways to demonstrate His power, I can but humbly submit, and I advise you to do likewise.

The kingdoms of Castile and Aragon greeted this announcement with delight. The bleakness of the Real Alcázar was broken by the arrival of circuses, strumpets, rogues, minstrels, and troupes of traveling players, one of which, the most renowned, set up a stage in the middle of the castle courtyard. The queen's curiosity was piqued by the name of their play, *Sleeping Beauty*, seeing in it another divine message that might signal an end to her problems, so she decided to grace the first performance with her dour presence. Thus spoke the narrator:

The origins of this tale date back many centuries. It began with the christening of a king's daughter. The king issued an invitation to all the fairies of the kingdom, who rushed to give the babe their finest gifts, but he overlooked one, the Wicked Fairy, who, despite this oversight, appeared at the party, ready to give her own gift:

—If she should ever prick her finger, she shall die.

Happily, one of the good fairies changed that curse for one less dreadful:

—She shall not die, but fall into a deep sleep, from which only a prince's kiss can wake her.

The terrified king ordered that every spindle and spinning wheel in the kingdom be destroyed, but he could not prevent the Wicked Fairy from disguising herself as an elderly spinner stumbling upon the little princess, who was curious about the sharp spindle, having never seen such an object before. She asked the old woman what it was. A spindle, said the smiling fiend. And seeing that the girl liked it, she gave it as a gift and vanished. Not knowing how to handle this strange object, the princess pricked herself and instantly fell asleep.

On hearing these last words from the narrator, Isabella and Ferdinand exchanged wary glances. The narrator continued:

The king commanded that the whole country accompany the princess in her sleep, so that when she awoke, she would notice no change in her surroundings. And so it was. All the people, and all the beasts, went to sleep. One day, by chance, a foreign prince happened to pass. Seeing the little princess peacefully sleeping, he could not resist the urge to kiss her, for she was the most beautiful creature he had ever seen. The princess woke and with her all the people and the beasts. Life in the kingdom resumed its happy time. The two were married, and in due course heaven blessed them with the arrival of a child, who promised to be every bit as beautiful as her mother.

All was well until, by sheer misfortune, their daughter met with the same fate. Once more, a father sent the country to sleep, and once more a foreign prince woke her with a passionate kiss. So it continued for many generations, so many that it was thought to be a hereditary curse. This was a wondrous discovery, since over time, the kingdom was much changed, and the people would no longer submit to such wanton laws as those compelling sleep without rebelling.

The kings adopted all manner of solutions to save their firstborns from the dread disease. One, for example, came up with a plan that, while not perfect, at least did not involve the populace. He invited the princes from around the world to visit the kingdom, and from them he would choose his daughter's future husband and heir to the throne.

Princes, charlatans, and adventurers came from the four corners of the earth with dreams of winning the beautiful princess and, with her, the crown and the kingdom.

The long line of suitors began their procession through the royal chambers, but none could wake her with his kiss. With growing unease the king and queen watched the tedious ceremony.

Half the pretendants had passed through when an angry commotion broke out in the middle of the line. The voices reached the king and queen, who came to discover the reason. The cause of the disturbance was the son of Brígida the cook, Daniel, who loved the princess. The two had been inseparable playmates since childhood.

—What is it you seek, Daniel? —the queen asked angrily.

—To wake the princess, Your Majesty.

The queen was touched by this pure gesture, but told the lad:

—That cannot be, Daniel, since you hold no rank or title.

—I make no claim to riches —said the boy—. I want only to wake the princess, because it pains me greatly to see her as though lifeless. Look on the faces of all these men, they desire naught but her dowry. The only reward I seek is to bring her back to life.

Faced with this selflessness, the queen was at a loss for words.

—That cannot be, Daniel —the king said.

Head bowed, the boy departed, and overcome by this refusal, he too fell ill. He did not eat, nor speak, nor laugh. Distraught at her son's sudden malady, his mother was so bold as to visit the royal chambers. Even as she entered, the last suitor laid a kiss on the princess's lips, to no avail.

—Brígida, how dare you venture unbidden into our private chambers? —the queen rebuked.

The real king and queen, that is to say, Isabella and Ferdinand, were following the fable's twists and turns with rapt attention, surrounded by courtiers as much spellbound by the actors.

—I would not have done so, Majesty, were it not a matter of great importance —Brígida replied.

—What has happened? —asked the king.

The poor cook did not know where to begin.

—Daniel is sorely ill, were it not so I would never have

dared speak out. I have a secret I must reveal: Your Royal Majesties remember the visit of the king of Neighboring Country some eighteen years since?

The king and queen assented.

—Well . . . Daniel is the fruit of that visit.

—How so? —the royal couple said in chorus.

—Ours was a fleeting, tender love. I dared not tell him of the child . . .

—Then he does not know? —said the queen, intrigued.

—No, Majesty. I vowed to keep the secret to myself, but I could not bear to hear my son admit he cannot claim the princess because he wants for royal blood, for 'tis not so. Though I may be a humble cook, Daniel's father is a king!

The fairy-tale sovereigns were stunned by this revelation.

—What say you? —the king addressed the queen—. There is nothing to be lost in the attempt. After all, none of the formal suitors has roused our daughter.

So it was that Daniel left his sickbed and swiftly ran to keep his appointment with the princess's lips.

He kissed her and, from his love, there sprang a miracle. To the delight of everyone, the princess woke.

In the epilogue, the fairy-tale king and queen extend an invitation to the king of Neighboring Country, who is recently widowed and without a son and heir. On his arrival, he is reunited with his beloved Brígida the cook and young Daniel, the unknown fruit of their passion. What followed was a double wedding: on one side, the woken princess to young Daniel, now a prince, and on the other, the king of Neighboring Country to Brígida the cook.

The room erupted with joy at the conclusion of the fable, and the courtiers applauded wildly. The Catholic queen stared into the distance, engrossed in her own preoccupations. When he realized the analogy between the fable and his daughter Joanna's unbroken sleep, King Ferdinand was furious. He wanted to order that the actors be arrested so he could discover who had told them about Joanna, but the queen enjoined him to do nothing. Once in their private chambers, Ferdinand gave vent to his outrage.

—This is unconscionable mockery!

—You, the ever prudent, diplomatic Catholic king, cannot see beyond the end of your nose —Isabella chided him with calm contentment—. Through these traveling players, God has made Himself manifest.

—What are you saying? Surely you do not intend that we send to every prince in Europe to come kiss our daughter?

—Give me time to collect my thoughts. —Until now, Isabella had always had her way—. These are extraordinary circumstances, so the solution, too, must be extraordinary —she said by way of explanation.

In the days that followed, the queen forgot her torments as she strove to finalize the details of what she hoped would be the solution to her daughter's lengthy slumber. Once everything was in place, she confided in her husband.

—I know this is madness, but I am reckless in my nature, as you know. The plan I have devised to rouse Joanna may sound absurd, and so it is, and if it fails we shall be ridiculed, but you know I do not care about such things.

—In the name of God, speak —said the king.

—As you can understand, it was divine providence that brought the players here in time, and with them the answer to our daughter's plight . . .

Ferdinand looked at her with interest. He would have preferred not to grasp the sense of Isabella's allusion.

—This was a fairy tale, Isabella, a children's story that should inspire only suspicion.

—Suspicion? The reality is that our Joanna has been asleep these five months past, and then, just as God ordained that I forsake my penance and seek pleasure and distraction, these traveling players arrive and, by chance, perform a play in which there exists a hereditary curse that dooms a princess to sleep until she is kissed by the right prince . . .

—If this preposterous curse were true, we should have known it sooner.

—All things hereditary are mysterious, they do not reveal themselves so easily.

—And what do you intend?

—That Joanna be kissed by the man who will betroth her.

—But Joanna will be queen, she cannot marry just anyone.

—I have already given it much thought. It would be in

our interests if Joanna were to marry Prince Philip, son of Maximilian of Austria, who, because of his mother's untimely death, is already ruler of Flanders and Burgundy. In him we shall find an excellent bulwark against our sworn enemy, the king of France. What think you?

—Excellent, but how do you plan to entice Philip?

—We shall announce his engagement to our daughter and invite him to come and claim his bride-to-be. Joanna has much to offer the young archduke. On the pretext that the Infanta is too young to undertake the arduous journey to Flanders, we shall have him come for her.

—It is most unusual, but we can try. And once he is here?

—We have him kiss her.

So, the Catholic monarchs resolved to assume the risks of this eccentric plan and dispatched an official delegate to Flanders to negotiate their proposal. The archduke accepted the proposed marriage and thanked them for the invitation to come and meet his new kinfolk.

Flanked by a large retinue of Flemish noblemen, Philip set out, and when the party crossed the Pyrenees, they marveled at the country's curiosities.

When, after several weeks, Philip arrived in Toledo, the king and queen greeted him as their son and personally escorted him to the chambers of the princess.

—Just now, she is sleeping —the queen explained—, but she will be overjoyed to wake and find you by her side.

Philip found this behavior charming and unusual. Indeed, it would have been unthinkable in every European court, but this being Spain, nothing surprised him.

Joanna lay waiting for her betrothed, luxuriously adorned and sleeping like a stone.

—She is most beautiful —said Philip quietly, amused by the lack of protocol.

—Yes —said the queen—. Kiss her. Be not afraid. After all, you are already betrothed.

Philip would not have expected this encouragement from such a puritan sovereign, but he was beginning to accept the constant surprises of Castilian life as natural. Even he, who was unaware of the importance of the kiss, could sense the air of apprehension. In a state of unspeakable tension, the king and queen watched and held their breath as Philip, somewhat self-consciously, bent toward Joanna's lips and kissed her. But once again, Isabella saw her plans crowned with success. Finally, after ten long months, Joanna opened her eyes, and her expression could not have been happier.

When she saw the handsome Flemish man gazing at her tenderly, she thought herself still sleeping.

—So . . . it was not a dream? —said the Infanta.

The queen could not contain her joy.

—What, my child?

—While I slept, I had but one dream: that a prince from a far distant land was coming to take me for his wife.

—And so he has. The archduke of Burgundy has come

to meet you before your journey to Flanders —her father announced—, where your betrothal is to take place.

The Infanta sat up.

She is enchanting, thought Philip as he heard her voice.

Joanna patted his cheeks as though to convince herself that he was real.

—Oh! I cannot believe it!

Once they were alone with their daughter, the royal couple explained the miracle worked upon her. The queen insisted that the rare disease should not be mentioned. All that remained was to thank God for His blessing and to inform Joanna of all that had happened in the world during those months, so that she might bear it in mind in her future conversations in Flanders.

Some days later, the young couple set out for Flanders, where their wedding was celebrated amid great jubilation. The festivities lasted many days, as the archduke was a great lover of entertainments.

The Spanish princess had to make significant efforts to adjust to her new country and her circumstances. It might have seemed a thankless task, but her boundless love was ample compensation.

Philip was the fulfillment of all her youthful aspirations. When she had opened her eyes after ten months of unbroken sleep, she had known that he was the love of her life, and as the day broke on their first night of passion, she made a vow to defend this lawful passion with her bare teeth if necessary.

She did not lack opportunities to prove this, since her husband was a constant temptation to the ladies of the Flemish court. Philip was frivolous and beautiful, a brilliant conversationalist and peerless sportsman. Often, when a tournament was held in his honor, he would spontaneously take part and he always won. In short, he was a captivating young man who loved to captivate, and more than once, the pleasure-seeking archduke allowed himself to be carried away by some momentary whim that afforded him the opportunity to discover an intolerant and wildly jealous Joanna.

So, many years passed, between violent fits of jealousy and unforgettable days of devotion, in the Flemish court. A series of events had changed the archduke's situation in Spain. Queen Isabella had died, and Joanna, without expecting it, because she had no head to think about such things, became heir to the throne of Castile. She and the archduke were compelled to travel to Spain, since the country was eager to fill the empty throne. Once there, Joanna quickly discovered the rival ambitions of her father and her husband. Each vied with the other, and she decided that if the reason for this petty rivalry was the throne, she would share it with neither. Joanna was her mother's heir and the only one the populace acknowledged and supported.

In the midst of these hostilities came an event that changed the course of everything. Philip fell gravely ill. During his last days, Joanna did not eat or sleep, and she cared little for her appearance and less still for her responsibilities as queen. For

Joanna there was but one life, and it was irretrievably extinguished at Philip's death.

Joanna could not accept her husband's death. There was not reason enough in the world to persuade her he had died, and so began her long torment. Ignoring her father's advice, she had her husband's body decked with flowers and jewels, since she wanted his reawakening to be joyful.

—But daughter —King Ferdinand said again and again—, you cannot spend your days and nights next to a corpse.

—A corpse? Philip is not dead, but sleeping. After all his ball games, he needs to rest. He partakes in too much exercise. And it is not so strange to sleep for months on end, remember that I too slept for almost a year.

—I understand your grief, my child, but you have many responsibilities that you cannot neglect.

—You deal with them. After all, it is for this you plotted and schemed. Who would have thought that Philip's sleeping would place you on the throne! Truly, life is strange. Tell the nobles that I am mad, perhaps you will be luckier now than before. Spread the rumor that I am living with a corpse, and thus you may win the throne of Castile. Nothing now matters to me, save my duty of staying by Philip until he wakes.

And indeed, Ferdinand was surprised to find himself in such auspicious circumstances.

—And tell the people of Castile that Philip is not dead, but sleeping, and as a dutiful wife I shall sit by him, and you shall take my place until he wakes.

Joanna's madness was obvious to Ferdinand, her father, and according to Isabella's will, only if their daughter were clearly incapacitated was he entitled to rule Castile. His grandson Carlos was a mere boy and living outside Spain. When Joanna died, Carlos would be king, but until then he had no rights. Although there could be no doubt that Joanna was mentally incapable, the Catholic king was unsure how best to act, fearing that, in a fit of despair, his daughter might take her life, in which case the regency would slip through his fingers and Carlos would become king of Castile.

For many days, Joanna waited anxiously for her husband's corpse to awaken. She did not leave his bedside for a second. But death was the most powerful rival the queen had encountered. When she realized that patience was not an effective course, she decided to act. The first thing she did was to transport Philip to Granada, where he wished to be buried. This is what she told her father.

—If he is still alive, he will know that I am taking him to his tomb and will try to wake so he can dissuade me.

Ferdinand could not avoid the beginning of this necrophiliac cortege. When they pitched camp for the night, the queen had torches set about the coffin so that the corpse would never be in darkness and, should he open his eyes, would find light. But the cortege never arrived in Granada. Ferdinand hatched a plan to put an end to this macabre spectacle. By dint of trickery, he confused Joanna and took her and her dead husband to Tordesillas. To fuel her obsession, the Catholic king had the corpse transported there and encouraged her to nurse him back to health. Once Ferdinand had ascended the throne, it was important that Joanna never return to her senses: if this should happen, all his machinations to keep the crown of Castile would be in vain.

In Tordesillas, Joanna lived out years of misery, madness, and mistreatment. As long as Philip persisted in death, Joanna, demonstrating her unshakable loyalty, would continue to be insane. And lest the queen regain her sense of reason, her jailers attempted to bewilder her, giving her false news of what was happening in Spain and Europe, such that if anyone should chance to listen to her, they would be convinced of her madness.

Some years later, Ferdinand died, but this news was not conveyed to Joanna. She could not have dreamed that she was now the most powerful monarch in all of Europe. On the contrary, ragged and decrepit, she lived like a woman buried alive. Just as death had ravaged her young and healthy husband, so life had her in its death grip, heedless of the misery and squalor of body and mind.

At this time, her son Carlos came home to take the crown. All the important offices of state fell to the hands of foreigners whose chief motive was to profit at the expense of the Spaniards and to enrich their houses and their wives in Flanders. Joanna had to be kept hidden, since she was the rightful queen and the people had to continue to believe she was an incurable lunatic. Carlos intensified her confinement and entrusted this delicate task to the Marquess of Denia and his wife. Since Joanna was not easy to control, her jailers did not hesitate to impose more brutal punishments. In truth, their aim was to hasten the queen's death, but that specter had a superhuman vitality.

After several years of horror, Joanna, whose only support was Philip's skeletal body, began to despair that he would ever wake. She had suffered too much during the waiting, and though her love was undiminished, she no longer had the strength to endure such suffering.

One day, she called her guard and asked her for a needle.

—It is not fitting for a queen to dress in rags. I shall sew my own garments.

Kindly and with mournful lucidity, Joanna lied about the use she intended to make of the needle, for in truth she cared not what she looked like.

Our queen has regained her wits, thought the guardian in fear and wonder.

After the woman handed her the needle and left her alone, Joanna pricked her finger several times.

—I wish to sleep —she said over and over to the jagged spirit—. I wish to sleep. If I cannot sleep, I do not wish to be in this world. Sleep will rid me of all horrors.

And she continued to prick herself.

When the guardian told the Marquess of Denia of the queen's request, he reproached her for complying without first consulting him. The queen was to remain secluded and insane. The least flicker of sanity was to be stifled and silenced.

The marquess visited Joanna in the cell and heard her say over and over that she wished to sleep forever, which reassured him that she was still far from reason, but he was to discover Joanna had retained her charisma. She was unaware that her son Carlos was now responsible for her incarceration.

Gently, the marquess asked her for the needle, but Joanna cunningly claimed to have lost it. During the days that followed, she had recourse to it, but the sharp point refused to satisfy her desire for escape. Finally, since her love for Philip was no longer enough and since life refused to quit her, she decided to surrender herself to the materiality of her time, assume her responsibilities, and enjoy her privileges. The first step was to see her father and gather together the nobles who had been ever faithful to her, to prepare for her return to public life.

—For this purpose, I demand to be robed as a queen. —She threatened the Marquess of Denia—. And if you do not do as I command, I shall have you executed.

The marquess pretended to accede to her wishes and disappeared from sight.

Ravaged by years of hardship brought about by the avaricious Flemish, the long-suffering people of Castile would have rather lived at the mercy of the whims of a mad queen than the tyranny of such fiends. Insane as she was, Joanna could do no more ruin to the country than they had done, and even then, it would not be from spite, but from her obsessive love for a dead man.

A great legend had been woven about Joanna, which, strange as it may seem, surpassed even her own momentous existence. In the eyes of the people, it was this legend that elevated her above her petty contemporaries.

To them, Joanna represented love, self-sacrifice, indomitable will, stoic endurance, and feverish imagination; all dangerous yet admirable and unusual qualities. The people of Castile sensed that their queen was a victim, as they were, of her son's manipulations. Eventually, their patience exhausted, they took up arms against the absent king and his undesirable ministers in the city of Toledo. Toledo was soon joined by Segovia, Zamora, Madrid, Guadalajara, and Toro. The despised Castilian people rose up against the abuses of their king and his Flemish friends. Paradoxically, at this time, Carlos, at the expense of the Spanish coffers, was defeating tenacious opponents for the throne of Germany, thus fulfilling the Habsburg dream of a universal empire. From this dizzying summit, Carlos could not have imagined that the specter of his demented mother would become the banner of the suffering people of Castile and that those few rulers still in Spain who had not gone to his coronation feast would be mercilessly slaughtered to cries of "Long Live the Mad Queen."

The *comuneros*, as the revolutionaries were known, marched to Tordesillas to liberate their queen from the fiendish Marquess of Denia, and found it difficult to see, in the gaunt and ragged figure, the daughter of the illustrious Isabella. Their emotions when they learned of the conditions in which Ferdinand and Carlos had kept the queen could not be put into words. At Carlos's express direction, Joanna still did not know of her father's death, nor that her son was about to succeed Maximilian of Austria, nor that Maximilian was dead. Still less could she have imagined that an invasion of foreigners had usurped the government, made a mockery of her people's honor, and decimated the economy. There were too many events to be absorbed at once, but to general surprise, the queen was undaunted and showed unexpected courage and determination. The commoners placed the government in her hands, and she accepted.

She apologized for her pitiful forgetfulness and disowned her dead father and her son for their cruelty to her and to her people.

Carlos was in Frankfurt am Main when he received news of the popular uprising and Joanna's reinstatement in Castile. In an incendiary letter, filled with reproaches, his mother made the situation clear: if he should return to Spain, justice would deal with him, as it had done already with all of his favorites. That justice would decide what future he deserved. A furious Carlos threatened with death his mother and all those who supported her, but time persuaded him that this was but an idle boast, and he resigned himself to exile.

(Joanna, who, to the end, was a loving mother, allowed him to return after a time. By then, Carlos had repented of his sins and gone into seclusion in the Monastery of Yuste, where he joined the order of the Hieronymites, ending his days in the odor of sanctity.)

Castile, having purged its honor in blood, embarked on a more auspicious era that began under the rule of Queen Joanna and her embalmed husband Philip, who presided from the throne next to her.

—At last he has got what he truly wanted —the queen confessed to the court about her rigid consort—, to wear the crown of Castile, though to his misfortune, it serves only as ornament.

The entire people and the court accepted this lifeless king. They respected and adored their queen, who in matters of government showed an unusual astuteness and intelligence. Finally, Joanna was living a life befitting a human being. She learned how to adjust to Philip's passivity and devoted all her efforts to ensuring the wealth and well-being of her subjects. History has devoted glorious pages to her and singles her out among all female presences of her time, transforming her into the symbol of all that is sublime and irrational in the Spanish soul.

THE LAST DREAM

When I step out into the street on Saturday, I discover that it is a bright, sunny day. It is the first day with sunshine and without my mother. I cry behind my glasses. I will do so many times throughout the day.

Having not slept the night before, I wander the streets like an orphan until I find the taxi to take me to the South Mortuary.

Although I'm not the kind of son who is liberal with hugs and visits, my mother is a crucial figure in my life. I didn't have the courtesy to include her in the name I use in public, as she would have liked. "Your name is Pedro Almodóvar *Caballero*," she once remarked, almost indignantly, "What's this nonsense of just calling yourself Almodóvar?"

Mothers always play it safe. "Some think that children are made in a day," according to Lorca. "But children take a long time. A long time." Mothers, likewise, are not made in a day. Nor do they need to do anything special to be indispensable, important, unforgettable, instructive.

I learned much from my mother, without either of us realizing. I learned something vital to my work, the distinction between fiction and reality, and how reality needs to be complemented by fiction to make life easier.

I remember my mother at each stage of her life, the most epic, perhaps, the period spent in Orellana la Vieja, a village in Badajoz, a bridge between La Mancha and Extremadura, the two vast universes I inhabited before I was engulfed by Madrid.

Although my sisters don't like me to bring it up, in those early days in Extremadura, our family's economic situation was precarious. My mother was always extremely creative, she was the most resourceful person I have ever known. In La Mancha, they have a saying: "She could draw milk from a stone."

The street where we lived had no electricity. Our floors were of beaten earth, it was impossible to keep them clean, any water made them muddy. The street was some distance from the town center, springing from a patch of stony ground. I cannot imagine the girls negotiating those slopes of slate in high heels. To me, it wasn't a street, it seemed more like a remote outpost in an old Western.

Life there was hard but cheap. By way of compensation, our neighbors turned out to be wonderful, welcoming people. They were also illiterate.

To supplement my father's income, my mother went into the business of reading and writing letters, just like in the movie *Central do Brasil*. At the time, I was eight, and usually it was I who wrote letters, and she who read out the letters our neighbors received. More than once, I glanced at the text that my mother was reading aloud and was astonished to discover that her words did not exactly match what was written on the paper: my mother embellished what she read. Our neighbors never caught on because her fiction remained always a perpetuation of their lives, and when the reading was over, they were delighted.

After I noticed that my mother never stuck to the original text, I tasked her with it one day as we were walking home. "Why did you tell her that she often thinks about her grandmother, and how she used to wash her hair on the front doorstep with the basin of water?" I said. "The letter doesn't even mention her grandmother."

"But did you see how happy she was?" countered my mother.

She was right. My mother would fill in the gaps in the letters, tell the neighbors what they wanted to hear, often things the writers had probably forgotten but would happily have signed their names to.

These improvisations were a great object lesson to me. They set out the difference between fiction and reality, and how reality needs fictions in order to be more complete, more pleasurable, more bearable.

For a storyteller, it is a crucial lesson. This is something I have come to understand over time.

My mother took her leave of this world exactly as she would have wished. And this was no accident. I found out today at the mortuary, she had willed it so. Twenty years earlier, my mother had told my older sister, Antonia, that the time had come to have her shroud made.

"We went down to Calle Postas," my sister says as we stand before the shrouded body of our mother, "to buy the robes of Saint Anthony, brown with a cord around the waist." My mother also told her she wanted a medal of the saint pinned to her breast. And a devotional scapular of Our Lady of the Sorrows. And a pin depicting Saint Isidore. And a rosary in her hands. "One of the old ones," she told my sister. "I'll leave the good ones to you girls" (she was including my sister María Jesús). They also bought a sort of black shawl intended to cover her head, that now reaches her waist.

I ask my sister about the significance of the black shawl. In the past, widows would wear a long black muslin shawl as a sign of grief and mourning. As time passed and their grief ebbed, the shawl became shorter and shorter. At first, it fell to their waists, and by the end, it barely reached their shoulders. Her explanation makes me think that my mother intended to leave this world in widow's weeds. My father died twenty years ago, but it goes without saying that there was no other man, no other husband for her. She also insisted that she be barefoot, with no stockings, no shoes. "If my feet are tied," she said to my sister, "you will loose them when you put me in my grave. Where I am going, I want to tread lightly."

She also requested a full requiem mass, not just a funeral service. We respected her wishes and the whole town (Calzada de Calatrava) flocked to "give us the nod," its term for offering condolences.

My mother would have been delighted by the number of bouquets and wreaths on the altar, and by the fact that the whole town came. "The whole town was there" is the greatest thing one can say about such an event. And so it was. And for that, I am grateful: thank you, Calzada.

My mother also would have been proud of how impeccably my siblings, Antonia, María Jesús, and Agustín, played the role of perfect hosts both in Madrid and in Calzada. I just allowed myself to be swept along, my eyes misted, everything around me a blur.

Despite the whirlwind of press junkets that is my life (*All About My Mother* is currently being released around the world; thankfully, I had decided to dedicate the film to her, both as mother and as actress; I hesitated a lot, because I was never sure whether she liked my films), I fortunately happened to be in Madrid and by her side in her last moments. All four of her children were constantly with her. Two hours before "everything" was unleashed, Agustín and I went in to see her during the half-hour visiting slot permitted by the intensive care unit, while my sisters sat in the waiting room.

My mother was asleep. We woke her. Her dream must have

been enjoyable and so engrossing that it did not leave her, though she spoke to us perfectly lucidly. She asked whether there was a storm raging, and we said no. We asked how she was feeling, and she said very well. She asked after my brother Agustín's children, who had just come back from their holidays. Agustín told her that they were spending the weekend with him and would have lunch together. My mother asked whether he had already shopped for food, and my brother said yes. I told her that two days later I was scheduled to go to Italy to promote my film, but that if she wanted, I would stay in Madrid. She said I should go, that I should do whatever I had to do. She was worried about Agustín's children. "What about the children, who will they stay with?" she asked. Agustín told her that he was not going with me, that he was staying. She thought that was for the best. A nurse came in, and in addition to telling us that visiting hours were over, she told my mother that she would bring her some food. "Precious little smoke will come of putting food in this body," quipped Mamá. I found the remark strangely beautiful.

Three hours later she died.

Of all the things she said during that last visit, the one that sticks in my mind is when she asked whether there was a storm. Friday was a sunny day, and some sunshine was streaming through the window. What storm was my mother referring to in her last dream?

Pedro Almodóvar Caballero

THE LIFE AND DEATH OF MIGUEL

Various relatives and future friends attend the birth of Miguel, all watching attentively as the gravedigger unhurriedly goes about his task. The faces of his closest family reflect the natural resignation and grief that attend such doleful affairs. Miguel, his name is known to everyone, will be born into tragic circumstances. This, too, is common knowledge.

From the first moment, it is possible to know how long the newborn will live. According to the capricious laws of nature, Life is a finite period, the span of which is determined at the moment of birth. The documents with which each individual is born, which spontaneously appear whatever the location, stipulate the date on which the cycle will end. For some it is sooner; for others, later. In this sentencing, none but Chance can intervene. This is one of the great mysteries of life. The age of the newborn is informed by the boundaries that mark his beginning and his end. For example, after his first birthday, a person born at forty will say that he has been alive for a year and has thirty-nine years remaining before his death.

No one has seen Miguel yet, the gravedigger's progress is slow. From what has been said, it seems that he will be born quite young. His mother knows this and can scarcely suppress her tears. From deep in the pit, the wooden coffin containing him appears. In accordance with tradition, the relatives reluctantly and lightly toss a handful of earth to greet the newborn. The parents are sobbing bitterly, one of the aunts comforts the mother with empty platitudes.

—No matter how long life is, it cannot last forever. In the end he, like everyone, will die a liberating death.

—I know my poor child will be born into tragic circumstances —the mother groans, her voice breaking.

—Don't think about that now —insists the aunt.

Between hushed sobs, the mother wails:

—To be born so young . . . Miguel never did anyone any harm.

The men charged with the exhumation use ropes to lift the coffin containing Miguel: this is the first phase of birth. The priest concludes the ceremony with a few prayers, wishing the child happiness in his future life while friends of the family shoulder the coffin and carry it to a hearse, which, in turn, will take him home.

The parents, various aunts and uncles, and Elena, a future close friend and the person who knows most about the circumstances of his birth, drive back to the parents' house together with some family friends. There, the farewells begin. Those leaving try to cheer the parents up, offering to help in any way they can. The mother looks at them, bewildered, she does not know what kind of help they mean, nor do they. It is simply a stock phrase everyone uses, like a ritual. The only ones left in the house are Elena, the future friend, and the aunt who had offered comfort.

The morticians place the coffin in the bedroom and unseal it. It is now possible to contemplate Miguel's stiff, marmoreal body.

There is a knock at the door, a lady has come and asks to speak to the mother.

—She can't talk to you at the moment —says Elena, who has gone to greet her.

—I assumed as much —says the woman—. Let me explain: I have an apartment for rent. Until recently, it was empty, and then suddenly today I found it filled with books, clothes, and various items that seem to belong to a young man. I looked for the accompanying documentation and found it, at which point I immediately assumed there had been a birth. It listed his parents' address. If you'd like to come and collect a suit or whatever you might need . . .

—I imagine that if the belongings you found do indeed belong to Miguel, he'll up and live there. I'll just come and fetch some clothes. But let me take a look at the document, because it might correspond to a different birth.

Elena reads through the document.

—Yes, that's him, his name is Miguel. If you've suddenly found the room full of his belongings, he must be about to be born.

—I know you —says the woman.

—Yes, we must have run into each other at some point.

—I thought as much. Do you need anything else?

—No, thank you. The only thing to do now is wait. Thank you for letting us know.

Elena goes back to the room where Miguel's corpse has been woken. Four candelabras stand at the corners of the open coffin. The mother comments:

—He's so young! He seems half asleep and he looks surprised and scared. My poor little boy. Have his belongings turned up yet?

—Yes —says Elena—, a woman just came by to let me know where Miguel will live after he's born.

—So, he won't be living with us? —The mother sounds disappointed.

—No.

—How long will he live?

—Twenty-five years. Here, look.

The mother hurriedly snatches the document proffered by Elena on which the dates of his Birth and Death are set down.

—I'd like to visit this apartment and see how he's going to live for the first few days —the mother says.

—There's no time —says the aunt—, and there's nothing you can do there. We have to hurry, it can't be long now before he's born.

As is customary, they have to sit vigil for the future being. Elena and the various relatives who have arrived take turns. The time drags, the night draws out interminably. The following day, a little more rested, though they have not slept, those still at the parents' house prepare for the final, inexorable stage of birth.

The clothed body of Miguel shows no distinguishing marks.

—What's to become of him, only twenty-five years old! —the mother suddenly shrieks.

—Let's undress him —says the aunt—. We'll put on the clothes sent from his apartment. There are no signs of violence, and at such a young age it would be unusual for him to be born as the result of illness . . .

The expression on his face is frightening. A rictus of astonishment and grief.

—Yes, poor thing! Let's undress him —sobs the mother.

Carefully removing his dark suit, they discover the bullet wound in his chest. Elena had already related some of the tragic details of the birth to the aunt, but somewhat confusedly. The mother weeps at the inevitable threat that hangs over her son. She wishes there were something she could do, her heart broken by her helplessness in the face of tragedy.

—With luck it won't always be like this —her sister reassures her—. After this tragedy, I'm sure his life will have moments of happiness and pleasure. Despite that grim expression, he's a handsome lad. He takes after your husband.

After stripping the body, they wash Miguel and leave him alone in the room. The end of the most painful part is approaching. All that remains is the actual birth. In Miguel's case, given his youth and the wound to his chest, this early stage is likely to be difficult, but for his relatives, life will go on, the pain they feel will abate, and at worst, they will be left with some level of anxiety over Miguel's fate.

It is difficult to know the details of his immediate future, but from the circumstances surrounding his birth, an educated guess can be made. And in Miguel's case these circumstances are far from comforting. That wound in his chest points to a gunshot that will shortly deliver him into this world, but no one knows where it will occur. Little time remains before the bullet that will birth him is fired. Much as they might try to keep his chest clean, the wound is still raw and tender. For those who have stayed with the parents, the wait seems interminable, and eventually all, including young Elena, decide to go home.

The mother is distraught. At length, some men come to collect Miguel, and at the moment they are separated, the mother screams wildly: —No, no, Miguel, no! —She knows what is going to happen. The men are taking her son away so that he can be born after being shot. The mother's repudiation reveals her utter helplessness, she can do nothing to prevent his tragic birth. Blood gushes from the wound. The men carrying away the lifeless body form a wandering funeral cortege. Heading down the street where Miguel's parents live, and through a dusty park, guided only by intuition, they walk aimlessly for twenty minutes, as though hypnotized or in a trance, until, suddenly, the corpse falls from their hands and, with a bizarre jolt, it rises. Once he is completely upright, arms wide as though he is dancing, Miguel lets out a bloodcurdling scream. This is the scream that the men have been waiting for, the primal scream that shows that Miguel is alive. The men who carried him here flee to a bar across the street. It all happens in a matter of seconds.

A man slightly older than Miguel, his face a mask of hatred, fires a revolver from the opposite sidewalk (next to the bar the men who carried Miguel here have just entered).

Miguel has just been born, he takes his first semiconscious steps. The wound in his chest has suddenly disappeared. Miguel starts life with the certain knowledge that something fatal is about to happen and that he will have no time, no way to avoid it. From the corner across the street, the man who shot him shouts:

—Leave her alone, leave her alone!

Who is this guy? Why is he shouting at me like that? I don't even know him, Miguel thinks, upset that the first moments of his life are so violent. Why is this man shouting at him furiously? Miguel walks toward him and threatens:

—Keep this up and I'll have you arrested!

—You won't have time. If you don't agree to let her be, I'll end you right now.

As he says the words, he nervously pats the still-warm gun in his pocket.

Miguel, having just arrived in this world, without the slightest experience, wonders what his relationship could be with this stranger. He is unbothered by the threats, but he is disconcerted at the idea that he has to do something to defuse the situation. Despite the man's visceral hatred, Miguel feels no ill will toward him and does not want to respond in kind. This is probably a misunderstanding, so he decides to keep himself in check.

—Calm down, you don't know what you're talking about.

—Leave her alone, go away. She doesn't really matter to you, you've got other things in your life, but she's all I've got. —The man roars, his voice is pleading and less forceful than earlier.

Miguel wants to tell the man that he doesn't know him and has no interest in his affairs, that he's just been born and is all alone, but seeing the man is volatile, he doesn't dare.

—What are you talking about, man? I don't know you. Who is this woman?

—You know perfectly well! Elena, who else could it be?

—Elena?

Miguel vaguely remembers who Elena is, but he starts to learn how to improvise. Although he still feels threatened, since the gun is still in the stranger's trouser pocket, he is less afraid than he was initially. He also remembers seeing this man in a photograph. As time passes, he feels more in control of the situation and begins to realize what his killer is referring to.

—You're crazy! —says Miguel to get him off his back.

—Give her up, I'm warning you, I'll do whatever it takes.

Some time ago this stranger was Elena's boyfriend. His name is Eusebio. In the days before the birth, she berated him so often for being the killer that, for Eusebio, shooting Miguel became inevitable. When he saw him standing across the street, having been carried there by four men who dropped him on the ground, some uncontrollable inner urge prompted him to draw the gun and shoot. No one can ever be certain of their future actions, but if circumstances dictate that you have a particular obligation, it is impossible to refuse, it is beyond your power. Life uses individuals as pawns, and through them, it unfolds. Because of his short stay among the living, all these things are as yet unknown to Miguel.

—I'll do whatever it takes! —Eusebio growls again.

Feeling much calmer now, though he has no reason to be, Miguel adopts an admonishing tone to get rid of Eusebio.

—If your girlfriend's left you, regardless of who she dumped you for, forget her and face the facts.

—I don't want to forget her!

The conversation ends up turning into a rambling dialogue, and Miguel begins to get bored. All he wants is to have a drink at the bar next door, so in the end, to get rid of Euse-bio, he gives in.

—Alright, yes, I'm going with Elena —he says, although he doesn't know the woman. With this admission, Miguel con-siders the conversation at an end.

—So you admit it —says Eusebio.

—I admit that I don't know her. Look, man, I've just been born, you saw it for yourself, and even if, objectively, my mind is working (not that I know what the hell objectively means), I'm still having trouble playing my part.

But Eusebio doesn't want to hear what he is saying. He is tortured by the strange conviction that Elena has been un-faithful with Miguel.

They go into the bar. Miguel's pallbearers are sitting at a table playing dominoes, but they don't say a word to him, as though they don't know him. Miguel is calm. He wants to shake off Eusebio, who trots after him like a dog. Abruptly, he feels so self-assured that he says point-blank:

—Alright, yes, we're going together.

—I needed to hear you say it —says Eusebio.

—Well, now you've heard.

—Elena told me that you were leaving the country to-gether, but I couldn't believe it.

Eusebio crumples. He is on the verge of tears. Miguel looks at the bulge of the pistol in his trouser pocket.

—Have you got a gun? —he says.

—Yes —replies Eusebio, surprised at himself.

—Why?

—I don't know.

—Could you just go away and leave me in peace? —Miguel says quietly as he orders a beer at the bar.

Eusebio suddenly walks out of the bar, constantly glancing back as though he is looking for someone.

Having finished his beer, and with the whole day stretching out before him, Miguel thinks about what just happened with the stranger and, out of curiosity, decides that he'd like to meet this Elena, who seems to be the root of Eusebio's madness.

He goes out and spends a few minutes wandering aimlessly in the customary manner of those who live in the City. He stops in front of a house by Chance (the one rule that governs the Life of fellow citizens). As he rings the doorbell, he has a momentary doubt. Maybe he is being foolhardy, but he is very young, so he doesn't know the meaning of recklessness. A woman opens the door and Miguel asks for Elena. To his surprise, a beautiful young woman appears and ushers him inside. She treats him with great familiarity, and he feels completely comfortable in her presence, as though he has known her a long time. All he can talk about is his unfortunate encounter with Eusebio. About the shooting, their heated conversation, and going into the bar. And the way Eusebio left, out into the street, glancing back over his shoulder as though searching for someone among the patrons. The look of a madman.

Without knowing why, he calls the young woman Elena,

and since she does not demur, he carries on talking to her as though she were the woman Eusebio had been talking about. From her reaction, he realizes that the stranger's fears and accusations were not as unfounded as he believed.

So he was right, Miguel thinks.

A distraught Elena interrupts his thoughts.

—Eusebio scares me, he's so aggressive that I'm afraid he'll do something crazy. You don't know what he was like when I told him we were moving abroad. But for months now, he's been living at his place and I've been living here. We haven't spent a single night under the same roof since he came back from Germany! But he acts like nothing has changed.

—Don't worry, we'll leave as soon as possible. It'll be easier for him to forget if he doesn't have to see us.

Since Elena seems genuinely alarmed, Miguel humors her. Besides, he finds this young woman attractive and so unthinkingly allows his youthful impulses free rein. His future is a blank slate, the easiest course is to let himself be swept along by circumstances if he feels even the slightest pull. True, he did not know her, but his first impression could not be better. They act like old friends, and the curious thing is that their sexual chemistry comes as no surprise to either. If she wants them to run away together, Miguel is not about to say no. If she throws her arms around him and kisses him passionately, who is he to say no? It is what he wants her to do. Elena says they have to leave as soon as possible, she doesn't like what has just happened with Eusebio. Miguel goes with the flow. It is glorious to be swept away by this beautiful woman.

Miguel realizes that, from the moment he was born, his existence has been an uncontrollable maelstrom tossing him this way and that. He feels lucky to have met Elena, he thinks he loves her, and from the first moment, they start to screw.

AFTER A WHILE, she suggests that they think about their relationship and go and live somewhere far from Spain. Paris, for example. He does not answer, he'd forgotten that she had already suggested this.

—It's strange how quickly I forget everything that happens to me. Important things like promising you we'd move to Paris together.

—You're still a child —Elena says—. I'm fifteen years older than you, it's normal that everything seems strange to you. You'll get used to the transience of things. One day, I'll vanish from your life too, and it'll be as though we'd never known each other.

—But we do know each other.

—Of course we know each other. But a day will come when you'll see me on the street, with Eusebio probably, and you won't even give me a second glance because you'll have forgotten all about me.

—I don't believe that, Elena. I love you and I have no intention of breaking up with you, let alone forgetting you. As soon as you settle things with Eusebio, we'll go away.

—There's nothing to settle. He's not part of my life anymore. But you need to be alert, Eusebio is completely obsessed with me.

—Who's Eusebio? —says Miguel.

—Never mind, forget him.

—I forgot him just now. Am I ill?

Elena gives him a gentle smile.

—No. What are you talking about?

ANOTHER OF HIS early surprises is that, spontaneously and without deciding to, Miguel finds himself writing stories that are short, powerful, and very vivid, revealing a prodigious imagination and sophisticated style. He is instantly obsessed with writing, and this is another reason for him to be with Elena, since she is his first and most important reader, his critic and editor. The moment he writes something, Elena is first to read it. She shows extraordinary lucidity in everything that relates to Miguel, she knows him much better than he knows himself. Over and above their shared chemistry, they both feel utterly free, with none of the responsibilities of a couple. Although they spend much of the day together, their relationship feels surprising and spontaneous to them, as though it were new. But the shadow of Eusebio lingers. He has gone to Germany, but still he comes between them, perhaps even more now than he did at first. With every passing day, Elena becomes more restless, more insecure.

—I need to talk to him —she says worriedly.

—Why? You've made things perfectly clear.

—He's very violent. You don't know him . . .

It is true that Miguel has long since forgotten Eusebio. The name still rings a bell when Elena mentions that she has a boyfriend in Germany called Eusebio. Could this be the same Eusebio? His memory is precarious, as is Elena's.

FOR NO PARTICULAR reason, Miguel and Elena begin to see less of each other, their dates are more infrequent. Although she still enjoys Miguel's company, she needlessly feels more attached to Eusebio. Before long, they see each other only by chance, with no prior arrangement, when they get together with mutual friends, and they very much enjoy these encounters. They don't talk about the past, nor do they yearn for the time when their relationship was much closer, when they were planning to move to Paris together. It is not that they had second thoughts, it is as if these plans never existed.

With his limited experience, Miguel begins to understand that the present governs everything. The present is surrounded by a sort of haze, a before and after in which memory still persists. Just that: a haze that extends the present moment by a few days forward and backward.

It goes without saying that Elena has not brought up the

subject of leaving Eusebio again, and the idea does not even occur to Miguel. Their meetings now are very infrequent, and when they do happen, Miguel and Elena behave like strangers who get along well.

ONE DAY, AT A friend's house, he finds a book of short stories by an author who shares his name, Miguel Castillo. On the dust jacket, he sees a photograph of himself, and leafing through the book, the stories feel familiar.

—Is this me? —he asks his friend.

—Of course! I already told you that I loved it and how much I'm looking forward to the next one.

Miguel looks at him, stunned. How could he have forgotten? He is a writer, he instinctively began writing shortly after he was born. And he has carried on doing so right up to this moment.

He has only to read some of the stories to realize that, although he writes with the same fervor as he did at the beginning, the results are less impressive than the stories in the book. To him, this loss feels inevitable. Since he was born, literature has been the most important activity in his life, and although this has not changed over time, the problem is not simply that his talent has not improved, but that it has deteriorated.

He is too young to understand that a sense of perfection is inversely proportionate to the passage of time. Despite this, he carries on writing with the same excitement.

While searching his bookshelves for something by Pessoa,

he finds two copies of his book. He didn't know he had them. Gradually, he is less surprised when he contemplates what his life has been. He has almost completely forgotten Elena: some days ago, he saw her and failed to recognize her. His friends did not remember this previous relationship either and introduced her as though this were the first time they had met.

After this introduction, he will not see her again. He doesn't know whether she will stay in Madrid or leave to go and join this boyfriend of hers. He no longer thinks about Elena, he does not miss her: Elena does not exist. After her, he has a number of different affairs, but none of them leaves a mark. Nothing leaves a mark. He feels orphaned, empty, though he has parents who occasionally demand he come and live with them.

He reads the stories in his book over and over, recognizing himself in them is a glorious feeling. He tries and fails to remember when he wrote them. The stories he writes now are not as good as those he wrote then. He cannot understand why: he invests the same discipline and passion into them.

He grows accustomed to not understanding what is going on in his life and learns to accept things for what they are. He has not made much money from his book, but getting it published gives him confidence.

BORED OF MADRID, and despite his parents' opposition, he moves to London. There he survives by taking any job he can find. After a few months, he moves back to Madrid, where he quickly publishes his first book. One day, he finds himself in an editor's office but cannot bring himself to ask what this means for fear of looking like a fool, although, perhaps he could explain that he's just a child . . .

—How old are you? —the editor asks.

—Twenty.

—At what age were you born?

—Twenty-five.

—You're still a child. In time you will get used to not understanding anything. Then you'll stop trying. You're at the classic stage of asking questions.

—So everyone tells me —Miguel protests.

—I can't explain basic things like the fact that, in order for a book to be published, it must first be read by the public, then bought, and only afterwards can it be written.

—Is it also necessary that I not recognize my own stories, or know when and how I came up with them?

—Of course! And don't look at me like that. Even if you're the author, you can't possess simultaneous awareness of all the facets of your own creations. In time, you'll find out when you wrote them, and how. Be patient, that's just how life is.

—But surely it's normal for me to ask.

—Yes, just don't expect people to answer. We'd spend the whole day explaining things to you.

Miguel is happy with the way the book has turned out, the trouble is that the real work comes later. He has to correct the proofs of his stories after the book has been printed, but this does not bother him. He enjoys such tasks and he begins to not care about the order in which he has to do them. The past fades into something dead, like a sun-bleached photograph, its image now hazy and faint, lost to evanescent shadow.

AS MIGUEL GROWS older, new hobbies replace old ones. This progress is inevitable, and the most recent stage is always the most captivating, the only thing that is captivating. He finds work as an actor in the cinema, which makes it possible for him to devote himself to his literary work.

For a time, he appears in shoddy, forgettable movies, but he doesn't care. He has no respect for the cinema and prefers to work in unimportant, artistically unpretentious movies. During this period, he wears his hair long, and in a lot of Spanish films, it's fashionable to stage an impromptu party scene where long-haired men dance like lunatics. These jobs help him to survive.

Since he was born, he has lived alone. His family lives in Madrid too, but he has always refused to go and live with them. At first, they seemed to respect his independence, but as time goes by their demands become insistent, and although he has never agreed to explain himself to them, he finds it increasingly difficult. Until the day comes when he is forced to flatly refuse to live with them so he can focus on his own Life. As a result, his parents leave Madrid to live in the country, where his father has been transferred for work.

Now freer, but with straitened means, Miguel has various experiences that he finds moving, despite their simplicity. He is surprised by his growing naivete, his concerns are more puerile, while his illusions multiply with time. His pessimism persists with age, but it loses its intensity, becoming weaker and more bearable. A few insipid affairs of the kind he would have rejected as a child are enough for him to feel deeply moved.

As he expected, the stories that he writes are of diminishing quality, although they still bear some resemblance to those he wrote as a child. The difference between them is vast, but he has already abandoned the mature style of his beginnings.

Strangely, he effortlessly contemplates how he is drifting toward ignorance and thoughtlessness.

Is it worth carrying on? he wonders.

Perhaps he is still waiting for a surprise. At some point, it occurs to him that the process might be reversible, that he could go back to being who he once was. But when he looks around at the people born before him and realizes that no one has gone back to their beginnings, he realizes that this will not be possible.

—It's a fact of life —someone tells him—. You just have to accept it.

—That's not a reason —Miguel protests.

—Of course it is.

Although I still struggle, I've long since accepted things as they are.

—Fact of life.

—Yeah, fucked off life —Miguel dares to say.

He does not want to be rooted in the past or obsessed with it because there is no past, only the present exists and, at that, only fleetingly. He has already learned that evoking the past is pointless.

HE IS SEVENTEEN years old, it is eight years since he was born. His problems are not over yet. His occasional acting gigs have petered out and he has to look for work in order to survive and study, since he has no money. Although he's lived in Madrid for many years, he finds that he knows almost no one, as if he'd just moved here, a little scared and overwhelmed by the vastness of the capital.

He goes to the province to visit his parents. As he expects, they do all they can to keep him there. Miguel knows that he cannot live with them, but he is afraid that his defiance will prove futile. Every day, he knows that he knows less. He decides that he has to do something to fight this forgetfulness, even though years ago he accepted it as part of life. Something of his unnatural rebelliousness still bubbles inside him. Just then, he gets the news that he has passed his baccalaureate. Miguel knows what this means: first you get your results, and then you are trapped by the expectations they set. This is how his family and their provincial town clasp him to their bosom.

Madrid seems farther and farther away, he dreams of going back but doubts he will ever get another chance. Having graduated high school, he finds himself presented with a prison sentence he cannot refuse.

While Miguel's parents are still dismayed by his constant rebelliousness, they keep a secure hold on him, since he is constrained by the interests of his age. They know that his posturing is not temporary, like that of other boys, but fortunately the most difficult period is over. He needed to grow older before they could force him to live with them. Family life is a prison and school merely an extension of that.

Slowly, Miguel bids farewell to the ideas that have accompanied him throughout childhood and adolescence, plunging him into this nebulous period of adulthood. He is saddened by how distant his childhood seems and longs for an impossible return.

Problems that he had abandoned in the past because he knew they were inexplicable now present themselves with a histrionic need to be resolved, and he morbidly indulges these obsessions without achieving anything beyond the foolish, fearful piety inculcated by the religious atmosphere at his school.

As in all the stages of his life, he has only two or three friends, in voluptuous intimacy. His literary activity is all but nonexistent, he writes only tender, maudlin pieces now. His resolve to continue writing has waned, and he is awaiting the imminent arrival of old age, which will spare him these pretensions with something akin to joy.

AFTER TAKING HIS Bachillerato Elemental, he spends the summer with his aunt and uncle in a little village. Though he has had a number of amorous experiences throughout his life, none of which Miguel remembers clearly, this is the summer he first discovers sex. Each new discovery brings with it an end to the desire that motivated it. After this summer he will have only vague, confused erotic experiences.

Having already begun the process of re-creating his recent past, the Bachillerato Elemental, he mainly preoccupies himself with movies and a few friends.

ELEVEN YEARS OLD. Fourteen years since he was born. Miguel has become a sad and solitary old man who is, as he always was, a little disconnected from his surroundings. His literary output, if it can be called that, is limited to a handful of poems that speak of his loneliness, or short essays inspired by his religious piety. He has lost the concept of quality, what he writes seems neither good nor bad to him. Given his lack of skills and means, Miguel is entirely dependent on his family. He waits only for old age and death.

Even now, he feels a latent spark of restlessness, but he no longer dreams of anything. His parents remember the child he was, and with each passing day, his helplessness makes them happier. The passage of time gives them peace of mind. Miguel belongs to them. The best period of his life is approaching, he too can sense this. His religious fixations appear to him as mere fantasies. He is a sensitive old man, the results in his final years of education are brilliant, and he feels increasingly affectionate toward his family.

Despite his advanced age, he continues to be regarded as a special character by the priests and by his classmates. His idiosyncrasies (he uses a rather affected vocabulary that seems inappropriate for his age), his fragility, and his poetic pastimes isolate him further, but he is used to that, his life has always been like this. It is at this point that he wins a writing competition at school on the prompt "the Virgin Mary." After this, a sort of poetic invocation, he writes nothing more. Literature, like so many other things, vanishes from his memory and his imagination. Not even at this advanced age, when men typically spend their final years playing games, does Miguel conform. In his spare time, of which there is much, he would rather do anything else. It is also at this time that he watches his last movies. Eight years before his death, he gets intense enjoyment from the cinema, as though he senses that it will soon disappear from his life. More than ever, for Miguel, cinema is now the other Life in which he would like to live.

As is customary, Miguel's parents are very excited about

his old age. The younger ones joyfully watch as his abilities begin to fail. Faced with his increasing ineptness, Miguel feels alone. It seems as though others, aware of what is happening to him, simultaneously try to hide it from him and make fun of it. Fortunately, old age is a comfortable and undemanding period with no pressing commitments. Miguel no longer remembers his past even vaguely, though he dreams about it.

Now he truly needs his parents, his helplessness and his dependence are growing every day. But this is not the only reason for their closeness, his affection for them has also grown.

It is still something of a surprise to Miguel that he has physically shrunk. He no longer goes to school, and he enjoys the kind of carefree, happy-go-lucky life he lives. The way that people treat him has also changed. Some people with whom he had no relationship in the past now hug him and bring him presents. Miguel, too, has become more expressive. All around him, his parents' friends start to talk about how much time he has left to live, they all consider his death to be a great event.

HIS VOICE HAS become more high-pitched. Two years before his death he can barely speak and struggles to understand others. Gradually his life becomes more sensory. He is fascinated by external stimuli: noises, images, and movements. Before long, he can no longer form words, he only occasionally utters a small cry. He lives happily in his own little world, his mother devotes all her time to him, and Miguel has only to allow himself to be cared for without needing to reciprocate. (But then, how could he?)

A few months before his death, like all those who are about to die, he is a tiny, insignificant creature. A little animal. Old age is like the cloister of a silent order. No one can know what he is thinking, what he is feeling, yet everyone dotes on him and makes curious gestures when they see him.

His mother had never been as happy as she is now that she can help him die. Miguel seems as much a part of her as a hand or an arm. The knowledge that nature will use her as an inexorable conduit for her son and their subsequent anatomical relationship make her think of him as part of her body.

The hour of Death is approaching. Some days before, the mother falls ill in preparation for the event. She lies in bed for two or three days, an unmistakable sign that death is approaching. Miguel spends the whole day sleeping next to her, his only nourishment over the past months has been from his mother's breast. When the time comes, the doctor helps him to die by placing him between her legs.

A few days later, the mother leaves her bed, swollen from the presence of Miguel in her womb. The most painful part is over. Slowly, over the course of nine months, Miguel dies in her womb.

Thereafter, no one will think of him.

CONFESSIONS OF A SEX SYMBOL

I want to write a story so the first thing I ask myself is what I am going to write, what subject is worthy of my efforts. And, I have to say, I've a great idea: I'll write about myself. Because, the way I figure it, why invent a character when *I* am a character, and why dream up an entertaining, exemplary story when I could tell *MINE*?

The history of modern culture is littered with interesting characters who've written about themselves, take Andy Warhol, for example. Everything he wrote is about him and his friends. Then there's Anita Loos (I've never known whether it should be pronounced *Loose* or *Lohse*), who, years ago, wrote a diary and it was so successful that they even made it into a movie. And, as she admitted herself, she never believed that the pages she wrote without the slightest pretension, like mine, were the best philosophy book ever written by an American. This is something that seems to happen when funny people talk about themselves: the result, rather than being a diary or a memoir, turns out to be a work of philosophy. The same thing happened with Warhol. He wrote a book about his own obsessions (*From A to B and Back Again*) and all the critics agreed Warhol had written a book of philosophy. It doesn't matter whether it was about lingerie, glamour, money, or fame.

All this makes me think that, right now, almost without realizing it, I'm a deeply philosophical chick. And I have to say I love it. Anita Loos invented an alter ego for herself: Lorelei. I think the reason she did it was because Anita was short and dark-haired, and she wanted to picture herself as a gorgeous, voluptuous blond. But I don't need to hide behind some alter ego. My name is Patty Diphusa, and I plan to sign everything I do with my name. But I should probably get down to talking about myself, because without realizing, I'm already half a page in and still haven't said anything.

Everyone knows I'm a porn star in the photo-novel industry. If you believe the critics, I'm an international porn star, a sex symbol, and personally I think they're onto something. But sometimes publicity gives only a partial image. Because, let me tell you, I'm *so* much more than that. Otherwise, I wouldn't be here, sitting in front of this typewriter, telling the world about myself.

When a girl is nothing more than what people say she is, all she can do is go to clubs and bore the guys desperate to bed her about herself, since they're the only ones who put up with that kind of pity party. Now, me, I go to clubs myself, and I talk to the guys about *LIFE*, but after a couple of years I've realized that isn't enough. This realization has made me some enemies, but, hey, that's the way it crumbles cookie-wise. Sometimes a person's importance is measured by the number of enemies she's made.

Like, the other day I went to a casting call and I met my main rival: Fool Anna. This is a girl who thinks that the world would get along just fine if I didn't exist. She can't stand the fact that I get picked to play the lead in all the big porn photo-novels in this country. She thinks it should be her, not me. Besides, she's completely neurotic, the injustice of the whole thing drives her insane. Because not only am I the favorite of the readers and the casting directors, but even specialist critics really like me. For example, reviewing my latest photo-novel, *The Black Kiss*, they said: "The script is flawed, the photography achieves the impossible in being worse than the script. But, Patty Diphusa is divine." And if my screenplays are drivel, just imagine the ones that she has to take. Absolute shit.

Look, you might think it's stupid, but I don't hold a grudge against Fool Anna, and when I can, when I'm in the mood, I always try to be nice to her. Like, say, the other day I bumped into her at a party. Fool Anna had taken one of those drugs that make you chatty and nice to people. Otherwise, she wouldn't have said a word to me.

—How do you get such a perfect tan? —she asked.

And me, well, I'm not a bitch, except when being bitchy is fun, so I revealed my secret:

—Rub yourself with lemon juice and oil before you sunbathe. It's truly amazing.

When it comes to secrets, I've got many. Though strictly speaking they're not secrets, I'd call them pearls of wisdom. Wisdom I've mostly learned directly from nature. Because I believe nature is a great teacher. For example, lots of girls have problems keeping their figure, and they also don't get much rest when they decide to go to bed just to sleep. I've found a perfect solution to these two major problems. It's called heroin. If you take a little heroin beforehand, sleeping is a real pleasure. And if you keep taking it, within a few weeks, without realizing it, you'll have lost a ton of weight, because one of the best things about heroin is that it kills your appetite. Problem is, if, like me, you're a get-up-and-go kind of girl, brimming with ideas, when you wake up and you want to start writing, you don't feel like it. You're feeling chilled and relaxed, why go hammering on a typewriter? So, you press a mixture of orange and lemon juice, pop a couple of powerful pep pills, and before you know it, you're working like a maniac.

But anyway, I was telling you about my rival Fool Anna. So, the day after the party she takes my advice to heart and she goes into the kitchen to whip up the suntan lotion. But she doesn't have any lemons, so she's about to head down to the grocery store to buy some when she has an idea. She doesn't feel like squeezing a lot of lemons, and she figures she can get the same effect using concentrate. That way she cuts out the hassle of lemon squeezing. I ran into her a few months later and it was *not* pretty. After taking my advice, she'd developed a rash that kept her out of circulation for a week. She wanted to kill me, because she assumed I'd done it with, like, malicious intent. It didn't occur to her that sometimes there's no substitute for nature, and freshly squeezed lemon is not the same as lemon concentrate.

—One of these days I'm going to wipe that slutty pout right off your face —she said the minute she clocked me.

To which I replied:

—I really admire you, Fool Anna. There aren't many women like you left, but you watch yourself, pretty girl. I'm godmother to a gang of pimps (that bit is true) and it'd be a real shame for a woman of your caliber to wind up strangled on a patch of waste ground.

You've gotta be tough with Fool Anna, she's a seriously dangerous woman. She's one of those girls who were born in Serbia, in northern Yugoslavia. Girls like that always have big secrets, and just when you least expect it, they turn into panthers. Anyone who's seen Jacques Tourneur's movie *Cat People* knows what I'm talking about. And panthers aren't just for window-dressing jewelry stores, a panther can be a pretty dangerous animal if it has half a mind to be. That's why I give Fool Anna a wide berth, because I know she's got it in for me.

Now, you might think a girl with my particular assets needs a couple of bodyguards. It's something I've thought about a few times, but the disadvantage of bodyguards is that even the really hunky ones are boring after a while, and by the second night there's nothing left to talk about. Because, and I don't know why, interesting people never become bodyguards. The day Bette Midler and Carol Burnett become bodyguards I might hire them.

So, about my latest success, *The Black Kiss*. I attended the premiere of the photo-novel in Valencia, where I have lots of fans, especially among the gays, which is pretty much 90 percent of the province. The two-day junket was exhausting, with tons of interviews and lots of dinners. By the time I got my stilettos back on the plane, I was shattered, because, though I'd taken a lot of speed, nothing wears you out more than blow-out banquets and endless interviews. So, I decided to sleep on the plane. I'd just closed my eyes when the man sitting next to me said:

—Excuse me, are you Patty Diphusa?

I cracked open an eye. The gentleman was in his forties and smiling. There were lots of workouts and lots of millions behind that smile. That was enough for me to answer:

—There is only one Patty Diphusa. And I am she.

Then, somehow the two of us ended up having one of those

amazing conversations that every civilized person dreams of having whenever they get into a vehicle of any kind.

—I'm a huge fan of yours —he said.

—Flatterer! —I swooned, although it's not exactly surprising to find out that a guy in his forties is a huge fan.

—I guess you're used to people telling you that —he insisted with a humility that gave him a sexy edge.

—Oh, it's something you never get used to —I said to put him at ease—. A girl can never have too much flattery.

He offered me a cigarette and carried on talking.

—I buy all your photo-novels. Your presence adds something different to the genre. You have something very special, something you rarely find in a photo-novel porn star.

—You mean my beauty and talent —I said, but he didn't seem to agree.

—I'm not sure. It's hard to explain.

I didn't want to come across as vulgar by pushing the point, but I wasn't about to put up with someone throwing shade on my work.

—It's beauty and talent. Take it from me. Or maybe you don't think I have those qualities?

—Oh, yes, of course.

At last, we were on the same page.

—So, what are you doing now? —he said.

—Talking to you —I said. As jokes go, it wasn't particularly dazzling, I know that, but some guys get freaked out when they realize they're dealing with a girl who's got brains, and great photo-novel actress that I am, I know exactly how and when to fake it. So, since we were being "funny," I bounced it right back to him:

—What about you?

He was in fits of laughter.

—Talking to you —he said once he had recovered from the fit.

Before we knew it, we'd landed in Madrid.

At this point, there were only two possibilities: we go our separate ways, or prolong the encounter. But I didn't want to be the one to make a move, mostly because I was wiped out, and exhaustion is one of the few things that can make me pass up a good catch. He made the suggestion. His car was parked nearby, and once he had suggested it, I allowed him to drive me home. When we got to the front door, I thought maybe it was time for me to make things easier for him.

—You know all about me, but I don't know . . .

—I am a businessman. One of the most important plastics manufacturers in the world —he said, like it was nothing.

—Plastics —I squealed—. I just *love* costume jewelry.

I was tired, but I invited him to carry my luggage inside. Even if I'm just going on a trip to Valencia, I usually take several suitcases full of clothes. Naturally, the gentleman was sweating buckets by the time he'd gotten them upstairs.

—I'll just rest here for a minute, if you don't mind. —That was his excuse for hanging around. This gentleman was particularly slow in making up his mind, I will tell you why later.

—Not at all —I said.

After that, things got hot and heavy. What I mean is, up to that point, we'd talked a lot, but in the two hours the business magnate spent resting in my company, we barely talked at all. He was too busy paying homage to three of the most important orifices of my organism. I'm not going to tell you which ones.

Over the following days, my work schedule permitting, there followed many more homages. Mr. Business Tycoon gave me several pounds of costume jewelry, for which I was very grateful. But something about the relationship bored me. Actually, at first I thought it was kinda sexy, but . . . You see, after a couple of hours of "entertaining ourselves," just when I was about to fall asleep or make a phone call, he wanted us to get down on our knees and beg God's forgiveness. And he kept on and on long after it stopped being funny. I told him so. Then he told me that he was married, that he was a devout Catholic, and that his religion didn't allow him to be friends with me. So I said, yeah, it was probably for the best if we broke it off.

It's pretty upsetting for a girl to see a gentleman she's just had a nice time with filled with remorse and promising God he'll never do it again. Then again, all I had to do was reject him and he came crawling back two days later to tell me that he couldn't live without me, that since he couldn't be my lover on account of his religious beliefs, at least he could still see me. Simply contemplating my beauty would be enough for him. He had even come up with a plan. His two kids had failed geography, and they had to cram for exams in September.

—Why don't you give them geography lessons? At least that way I'll still get to see you.

—But I don't know the first thing about geography —I said.

The tycoon went back to his big house very sad. I went back to work, but by the end of the week I needed a break. Because, aside from my usual work, I'd been recording an album, a demo my friend Queti Pazzo says will be released soon. Queti started out with me in porn, but she had serious problems with her figure. She started popping every kind of amphetamine she could lay her hands on, but even then she could barely control her appetite. Now she doesn't care anymore because she's decided to give up porn and devote herself to music. Sex means nothing to her now. Her real hobbies are fatty foods, soft drugs, and rock and roll. When it comes to fats, her favorites are bacon, Galician empanadas, and tripe. With drugs, she keeps telling me "hard" drugs are *so* passé, that "the latest thing" is soft drugs, but at, like, OD levels. In other words, she smokes a pound of weed before leaving the house, and when she goes to a club, she'll drink, like, four quarts of alcohol (she considers alcohol a soft drug). All this, together with entire bottles of Minilip, Bustaid, and Dexedrine. She's not trying to lose weight anymore, but she still takes amphetamines out of force of habit.

So, the other day, we were in one of those nightclubs that have a restaurant upstairs, waiting for Queti to be served the second banana split and they're playing "Controversy" by Prince so, over the bass line, we started improvising a rap. It was something like "Suck it to me. Suck it to me babe. Suck it to me. Suck it to me now. After dinner. Before dinner. After lunch. Before lunch. After breakfast. Before breakfast. After flan. Before flan. Suck it to me," and so on. We really got into the groove and I have to admit it wasn't half bad. She said we should record a single. Side A: "Bloated by Fats" (referring to her face), Side B: "Cheekbones by Drugs" (meaning mine). Since she's decided to be fat, Queti has lost the ability to appreciate great cheekbones like mine. The single more generally would be called "Pure Trash."

So, what I was trying to say is that that weekend I wasn't planning on being there for anyone or anything, except heroin. I wanted to spend two days and two nights spewing and sleeping. You guys get what I mean. But the phone wouldn't give me a moment's peace: the drawback of being a bona fide sex symbol, who also knows how to behave in public and can string a sentence of more than three words together, if required.

The first call was from my sister. Her daughter was making her first Holy Communion and she wanted me to come, maybe not to the church bit, but at least to the lunch at Salones Hiroshima, where she'd booked a table. Then there was a call from some feminists asking me to take part in a conference about the aesthetic challenges of the woman of the future. The Prosperidad Neighborhood Association was organizing a local bazaar and wanted to offer me as a prize to the winner of the sack race. I also got a call from the Association for the Spanish Victims in Nagasaki (the staff of the Spanish House stationed in Nagasaki, who died because of the bomb). They're organizing a charity auction with proceeds going to the victims' families. Bárbara Rey, Silvia Aguilar, and Adriana Vega have all said they would come, and they'd very much appreciate it if I graced the event with my presence. I said no to everyone. Then the phone rang again. I decided this was the last time I'd pick up. A long-distance call from Honolulu. Ricardo Morente, son of Banca Morente, inviting me to come out for the weekend.

—I'm tired, Ricardo —I moaned.

—You can sleep as much as you like here. The view is to die for, you'll *love* it —he said to persuade me.

Long story short, I agreed, but I warned him that all I planned to do was get wasted and sleep. He said no problem. Ricardo Morente was the only sensitive guy in a family of bankers. By which I mean he's queer. When his parents worked out that this was irreversible and that Ricardo wasn't willing to live the life of a monk, they offered to buy him a mansion somewhere secluded, far from the gossips of Madrid, where he could live however he pleased without bringing dishonor to the family name. Honolulu, apparently, is far enough.

I slept through the whole flight. At the airport Ricardo

was waiting for me with his Italian houseboy (the cousin of an Italian ex-boyfriend). I arrived in the same state I'd left: totally numb. But Ricardo toasted every blunder and told me that I was amazing, divine, and wild. Coming from him that's a real compliment because, and I'm not sure why, billionaires have to go to ridiculous lengths to have as much fun as normal people, especially the ones who have a vocation to be an artist but no talent whatsoever.

You could say that I touched down straight onto the bed. Ricardo Morente insisted on showing me the scenery and all the things that make Honolulu different from Madrid. I told him everything was wild. I don't know if he registered my lethal state.

As soon as we got to the mansion, I snuggled into bed and started to get wasted. I mean, that was the reason I'd flown all this way. But I couldn't help socializing just a little. I think I remember most of the houseguests and most of the servants parading before my drug-addled eyes. Ricardo is very democratic when it comes to servants, they're usually as attractive as the guests, if not more so, and they're allowed more or less the same freedoms. The great thing about Ricardo Morente (aside from the fact that he allows you a certain autonomy) is that he has the finest drugs in the world.

I stayed a whole week, and though I intended to keep a low profile, several of the native houseboys went crazy for me. It's funny how things you don't give any importance to later turn out to be very important. One night, while I was smoking a spliff in Ricardo Morente's bedroom, he took out three chokers of fake diamonds and told the youngest and handsomest houseboy to choose whichever he wanted. The next day, the houseboy came to my room to see me off as I deserved and gave me the choker. I didn't dare refuse it, and I couldn't explain to him that I prefer wearing plastic to cubic zirconia. So, I took it and I promised to think of him whenever I wore it. And that was that.

Back in Madrid, I found out people had been trying to track me down to make a photo-novel, *Sows*. In the plot, I'm a girl who's living on the outskirts of Madrid, my father has a farm rearing pigs, and I've spent all my life around them. My father hires a farmhand to help me with the work and the farmhand falls in love with me and my father falls in love with him, which complicates things a lot, because while I don't have the hots for the farmhand, I sure do have a thing for pigs. I've just never known any other kind of love. Just as he's about to propose to me, I confess my bestial tendencies. And before he has time to be heartbroken, my father shows up, punches him, and kills him. I flee in terror, leaving my father with the dead farmhand. I'm hitchhiking, and I get picked up by a guy. After talking to him for a bit, he comes to the conclusion that I'm his daughter. When I was a baby, the nanny sold me, and no one ever heard of me or the nanny ever again.

As you can tell, it's the kind of story that completely falls apart unless it's rooted in a great performance. I was the perfect actress, but when they couldn't get hold of me, they got in touch with Fool Anna, who was delighted because, for once, she'd be stealing a part from me. But unfortunately for her, at the last minute they found out I was back and once again poor Fool nearly choked on her rage. If I'd known what was going to happen next, I'd happily have given her the part. I got home after a long, hard session with the pigs (surprisingly better actors than I expected, but a bit of a pain in the love scenes), opened the door of my apartment, and from behind I heard a terrifying roar. I turned around and saw Fool Anna transformed into a panther, and she looked pretty pissed. She skulked toward me in that elegant, menacing feline way.

—I've got a gift for you, Fool Anna —I said—. Don't rip me apart until you've seen what it is.

We went inside and I made a beeline for the fake diamond choker the hunky Hawaiian houseboy gave me. All things considered, I'd rather he was here to protect me, but as it was, I had to use my greatest weapon: my ingenuity. Growling in a way that made my hair stand on end, the panther allowed me to slip on the necklet. She looked at herself in the mirror and I think she liked it. I breathed a sigh of relief. But this was turning out to be a bumpy night. There was a knock at the door. I opened it and I found myself face-to-face with a guy who was twelve feet tall and all muscle, and who happened to be carrying a gun. Something made me think my natural assets weren't going to be enough to persuade him that this was no time to be bothering a working girl. With one hand gripping my throat and the other aimed right at my heart, he said:

—Where's the choker?

I was petrified with fear. I didn't know what to say. With a flick of his wrist he left me sprawling on the floor. As soon as the panther heard him mention the choker, she pounced, wolfing him down in the blink of an eye. It took me four hours to clean the place.

Two days later, his body was found on a vacant lot where I'd dumped it.

This is how I found out that the hood was working for the Morente family. Ricardo called to tell me the rest of the story. Turns out his grandmother, who adored him and accepted him for who he was, had given him a genuine diamond choker. Against his mother's wishes, he'd taken it to Honolulu, but only after having two copies made and reassuring his mother he'd show off only the fakes. But that night when I was staying, he showed the houseboy all three (including the real one) and told him to choose. Without realizing, the Hawaiian hunk chose the real one, the one he gave me. The day after I flew home, Ricardo's mother called and asked to borrow the choker for an exhibition of the family jewels. Ricardo discovered he'd given the *real* one to the young native. When he asked to borrow it back and found out the kid had given it to me, he flew into a jealous rage, which is a whole lot more hysterical in millionaires than in us mere mortals. He told his mother I'd stolen it and asked her to get it back and return it to him. If that wasn't bad enough, the guy who got killed by the panther was the brother of the Italian ex-boyfriend Ricardo had when he was young (the boyfriend's whole Italian family were hand in glove with Banca Morente), and so in a way no one could have predicted, the whole incident blew up into this huge international conspiracy. Because the Italian ex-boyfriend's family would not rest until they'd avenged the guy who'd been murdered.

I was scared to death. What could I do? I'm famous, I'm easily recognized, and here I was, cornered. Then, I had an idea. I called the plastics tycoon, took him to a hotel, and gave him the opportunity to pay homage to three of my most important orifices, then before remorse set in, while he was telling me how he was crazy about me and how I could rely on him for *anything*, I said:

—I think teaching your kids geography is an amazing idea, but due to my life circumstances, I'm completely ignorant. But that doesn't mean I can't learn. Why don't you buy me a round-the-world ticket? I could learn everything there is to learn about geography, sort of hands on. That's how I learned what little I know about *Life*. I'd be the best teacher for your kids, because they'd learn things from me no other geography teacher could teach them.

And I convinced him. I got him to buy me some new clothes so I didn't have to swing by my apartment to pick stuff up, and now here I am at the airport ready to take on the world.

Can I just ask all you book publishers, film directors, TV producers, etc., to be a little patient before marketing my memoir? Because I *KNOW* you'd all be gagging to buy the rights from me, but I need to spend a year traveling the world to see whether the Italians will get over their thirst for revenge. Just imagine all the things that could happen to me after I leave Madrid. I promise I'll write everything down. Because in writing these pages, I've discovered that I love being an author and a philosopher. The career of a drug addict sex symbol is bound to come to an end sooner or later, but as a writer (after a few months in rehab), I can live as long as state-of-the-art medical science allows.

I'll travel, I'll live, and I'll write, and I promise to tell you guys *everything*. My life has no meaning unless I can share it with others. With all of you.

BITTER CHRISTMAS

Saturday

When I woke up, I looked from the living room out to the veranda and saw Beau, arms and legs fused to that infernal contraption the Body Treck. The way he mastered it was a joyous sight, his every muscle taut, his perfect abs, his powerful and sinewy legs and arms, arms that, only a few hours ago, enfolded me in bed. It's glorious to watch, unbeknownst to him, as he sweats, and to admire the beauty and vitality that radiate from his body. In my hands and feet, the same contraption becomes an implement of torture. The sight of me panting for breath, jerking my legs, running nowhere is pitiful.

Beau spent all morning sleeping in the house with me. We spent last night in the emergency room.

Friday (The Day Before)

First thing yesterday afternoon, I started to get a splitting headache.

I popped the first painkiller and the second only hours later. That night, I launched a second attack, swigging Nolotil, my ultimate and most reliable weapon against the sort of persistent headache that starts in the occipital area and spreads until it covers my whole skull like a cap. With a headache like this, you can't watch TV, chat on the phone, read, work on your computer, listen to music, or travel by car. I retreat to the bedroom and lie on my bed in the dark while Beau watches TV, keeping a watchful eye without smothering me.

As I lie there in the silent darkness, a different feeling emerges, one that is distinct from the pain though the two merge the way a landscape merges with fog until it completely disappears. In my case, the process is the reverse: a powerful wave of nervous energy surges across my chest from left to right, then down my legs to my knees. My entire body is throbbing violently, and if it carries on, I'm afraid that it may end up exploding. My nervous system is completely out of control. I feel a burning sensation at the roots of my hair, and a sudden wave of heat sets my face ablaze.

I try to convince myself there's nothing wrong with me,

but the panic attacks are getting longer and longer and the pauses in between shorter and shorter. Time seems to drag on forever. I run my palms over my body, trying to grasp (or at least locate) the disembodied evil pressing on my chest in a way I can't describe.

It's the long weekend at the beginning of December and for the past two weeks an unseasonable Christmas has been sweeping through the city. Midnight comes. After hours spent struggling with the panic and the headache, I decide to go to the emergency room. Thankfully, Beau is here with me. I don't even want to think about how I'd have coped on my own. Beau doesn't say much, and I am grateful for that. At times like this, what's important is just to have someone there, keeping you company, the way pets do.

The Emergency Room

As soon as I get there, I register at the desk. Once they've put me on a bed, I lose sight of Beau.

They do a superficial examination and hook me up to an IV. The first bolus of analgesic has dripped through but the headache refuses to go away. I can clearly feel the war raging inside my head and I echo the onslaught.

My whole world has shrunk to an area that starts just above my neck and extends over the top of my head like a skullcap. The doctor on duty, a foreign guy with a nervous twitch in one cheek, advises me to stay overnight for observation. This was something I hadn't counted on, but the pain is so bad I quickly get used to the idea.

While they're trying to find me a room, I go out to the waiting area to look for Beau, but he's not there. I find him standing outside, despite the bitter December cold and even though he doesn't smoke. He hates hospitals, but he doesn't say anything. I tell him the news. I can tell he's exhausted, but he's determined to stay with me. He was working last night.

Beau is a fireman, and he also moonlights as a stripper in a club, but he's not your typical himbo: he's not body conscious, and he can't do a sexy, seductive dance. I think that's what people like about him when he's onstage. Besides, he's got the patience to put up with all the squealing bachelorette parties. I first met him when me and my friend Patricia were looking for someone to star in an underwear commercial. I took the photos and she designed the campaign. He and I hit it off during the shoot. And we spent that night together as though it was the most natural thing in the world. It was the first time this had ever happened to me. I'd never gotten involved with someone I'd been photographing a few hours before.

Back at the hospital, they put us in a private room. I am in the bed and Beau is on a blue sofa. I tell Beau that I know this place. Ten years ago, I shot some of the scenes for my second (and final) film in the corridors and two of the rooms on the very floor where we are now. One of the rooms was on the left of the corridor, the other on the right. In the movie, the character on the left died, the one across the hall survived. I'm not superstitious, but I'm glad they put us in the room of the character who survived.

I haven't done much cinema, only two films. I earn my living from advertising, but I've always believed there's something prophetic about movies. That's why I'm happy here, in the survivor's room.

I'm tossing and turning in the hospital bed. I'm very fussy about pillows (especially when I have a headache) and the one here feels like it's stuffed with stones that are digging into my neck.

I fight with the pillow, trying to find some way to stop it hurting so much, but I can't. Beau helps me find new positions for my head. In the end, the most comfortable is resting it on a blanket he has expertly folded. He's good at making improvised pillows. He's also good at mixing cushions and pillows. He's something of an expert, he looked after his sick father for the last years of his life.

They carry on pumping me with drugs through the IV.

Just as I finally drift off, a nurse comes in with breakfast. After all the effort it took to get to sleep! The headache has almost gone, though it's still lurking in the background, refusing to leave completely or disappear without a trace. I pretend everything's fine so they'll discharge me.

Saturday Morning

We get home at ten o'clock and go to bed. The long weekend has emptied the streets of pedestrians.

Bed is the space where Beau's body dominates everything. Here, with his arms wrapped around me, he confides all the things he didn't tell me during the night. He tells me that he hasn't set foot in a hospital since his father died two years ago, which is why he felt uncomfortable in the waiting room. My skin is grateful for his presence and he can sense this. Beneath the sheets, our bodies understand each other, as they have done since the moment we first met last summer.

Saturday, 3 p.m.

At three o'clock, I get up, dazed, wander into the living room, and look through the glass doors onto the veranda that serves as a gym and greenhouse. Beau is doing a workout on the Body Treck (I think I mentioned that at the start). He looks as though he's riding it, his body radiates health and vigor. For a few minutes, I gaze at him in awe. He looks at me, he smiles, and with my right hand I give him the same little wave the Pope gives to waiting crowds. Beau asks if I'm alright, I say yes, but it's not really true.

Evening, Night, and Early Morning

It's getting dark. Beau decides not to go to work so he can stay with me.

Although I don't tell him, I'm feeling sick again. The burning on my scalp, the palpitations, the feeling that my nervous system is completely out of control. I'm relieved to know, from what the doctor told me, that in cases like this the idea of death is completely subjective as long as you can manage not to throw yourself out of the window. Beau is on the sofa in front of the television watching a DVD. But I walk around the house several times just to keep myself moving. Thankfully, it's a big house. I avoid sitting down. If I sit still, the panic mounts, so I'm constantly running to the kitchen, the bathroom, the bedroom. I put some stuff in a storage room. I rearrange some books, take some out-of-date notes from the desk and toss them in the wastebasket. Then I go back to the sofa. I always go back to the sofa, sit next to Beau, put my arms around him, or lay my head on his chest for a while. I find it comforting. Trying to make it sound unimportant, I tell him the "twinges" are back, but they're not as bad. This is a lie, they're just as bad as before.

We go to bed early. I pop some of the Imigran they gave me in the hospital for the headache. And something to help me sleep: a cocktail of antidepressants and tranquilizers. My mouth opens, but I'm not sleepy. I'm wide awake.

I am surprised that the anxiety and tension in my head are allowing me to think more clearly. I even jot down some ideas for a future story on the blank pages of a short story collection on my nightstand. Writing keeps me distracted. I carry on scribbling on the back flaps of the book to keep my mind occupied. I can only write about what is happening right now (I've no ability to imagine). Meticulously, I detail the physical sensations of this instant. I do it sitting up in bed. I write a painstaking account of my two days violently struggling against migraines, tension headaches, and anguish. I even try to create a character out of what is happening to me, to transfer the panic and the pain, but it's impossible. Migraines and panic do not make for interesting cinema because they're not linked to action, a character suffering from them does so passively.

I finish making my notes and lie down again. Beau is already asleep. I admire his ability to fall asleep. It's something I lack. I admire and envy people who can fall asleep the moment their head touches the pillow.

Feeling the presence of such a beautiful animal sleeping beside me is deeply moving. Things would be much worse if I were on my own, as I've said. But I can't spend the whole night gazing at Beau. I allow my eyes to wander over his body, unhurriedly, as if it were a landscape. I turn the light off.

The landscape of Beau's body now exists only through touch. The darkness doesn't help me fall asleep. I turn on the light again. I try to read the book by Rubem Fonseca whose flaps I scribbled on minutes before. The book is called *Secretions, Excretions, and Madness*. I can't concentrate. I can't understand a single sentence, all I know is that it is about God and human feces. I'll read it when I'm better, but for now I put it back on the nightstand.

Once again, I feel overcome by bouts of panic. I do deep breathing exercises. Beau is still asleep. Beneath the duvet,

I touch his arms, his waist, the outline of his buttocks, his chest, now I run my hands all over him. I caress him, I embrace his brawny body to avoid tipping into the void. In the silence of night, my unease grows, the evil that I cannot name rages inside me whenever I lie down. I don't know why, but when I'm lying down I am more defenseless.

I glance at the clock. Just after 11 p.m. I consider going to the ER, but reject the idea. Last night, they managed to alleviate the headache, but the other symptoms have just gotten worse. I should have seen a psychiatrist. I should call a psychiatrist, but I don't know any. Especially not at this hour.

I remember Gabriela, a friend with a frenetic social life (she owns a restaurant frequented by politicians, designers, artists, and those who aspire to any of these three vocations), introduced me to a psychiatrist during a dinner at her house a while ago. I remember she's having a dinner party tonight. I was invited, but I flaked and said I couldn't go. I resist the urge to call her. I can hardly see myself pouring my heart out to her. Besides, Gabriela invariably ends up getting me into trouble and tight spots. (I may not have mentioned it before but, even though I've made only two films, I'm a bit of a cult director and the rare members of that cult are artists who go to Gabriela's dinner parties.)

I decide to call Patricia. She's had enough problems to require specialized help, although the real work needs to come from within, and she's been unable to find a workaround. There was a time when Patricia suffered more than I did. I know this because she used to tell me everything, but now I get the impression that she feels ashamed of herself and doesn't tell me anything. She has a phobia about breaking up with her husband, even though she thinks about it every day. (I find this deeply infuriating, but I respect other people's phobias.) Patricia goes to bed late, she's a graphic designer (we've worked together many times; as I mentioned, I was with her when she went to the strip joint looking for an underwear model and we discovered Beau). Patricia is one of those people who can concentrate better at night, and it also fills her long periods of waiting.

I call Patricia. She picks up, and it turns out that she knows more than one psychiatrist, but not well enough to randomly phone them in the middle of the night on a long weekend. With her usual calm, my friend offers a categorical diagnosis: what I'm going through, or rather what's going through me, is called generalized anxiety or panic disorder. She knows all about it, she took it for granted that I did too. It occurs to me that my life hasn't been so bad. She recommends a 0.5-milligram sublingual tab of Trankimazin.

It's a particular tranquilizer I don't happen to have. I am a newly anxious person. The headaches are something I inherited from my father's side, but when it comes to anxiety and panic attacks, I'm a rookie. The meds Patricia recommends can be bought only at a pharmacy on prescription.

—Go to your friend Gabriela's —Patricia suggests. —I'm sure she'll have Trankimazin tabs.

—I'd already thought of that but gave up because of Gabriela's hectic social life —I say—. Besides, she's having a dinner party tonight, and I already told her I couldn't go.

—I think it's the quickest solution, it's either that or go to the emergency room.

—I went there yesterday, but we didn't talk about my anxiety, just the headache.

—Go to Gabriela's, it's the quickest solution —she concludes.

Gabriela

I take the plunge, give Beau a blow job to wake him up, and tell him I'm having a panic attack and that we need to go see my friend Gabriela, since she'll have the drugs I need.

Still drowsy after his pleasurable awakening, Beau takes a moment to work out what I'm saying. It's hardly surprising.

While we're driving there, I explain that I'm a bit scared of Gabriela and that it would be best if he goes upstairs alone, because if she sees me, she'll insist I stay for the party, she won't believe that I don't want to do a line of coke, and she won't let me out of her clutches. Gabriela knows Beau because she's seen him with me a couple of times. Beau doesn't really understand why I don't want to go upstairs.

—It's a long story —I say—, but believe me, it's for the best.

In the end I explain the whole thing to Beau: you know how I'm a bit of a cult director, well, Gabriela always ends up trying to hook me up with someone to make a documentary, or something . . .

I realize that I'm in no fit state to explain things clearly to Beau. But it doesn't matter, he's willing to go upstairs and grab the Trankimazin, but first I have to phone Gabriela and let her know that Beau is going upstairs on his own, without mentioning that I'm downstairs, on the pavement, outside her door.

Gabriela shouts back, the party is very lively.

—Amparo, *darling*, I'm so glad you decided to come. I was about to call because I've just been talking to Barenboim about you.

—I can't come, Gabriela, but listen, I'm going to send Beau over. Could you give him a couple of Trankimazin? You've got some there, don't you?

—Of course I do, and cocaine and a splendid dinner. Barenboim has been missing Argentinian *milanesas* so I've made lots. And I know you love them.

—Yes, I do.

—And we've got ice cream. So, you'll come, won't you?

—No. I'm sending Beau, my boyfriend. I'm having a panic attack and I need some Trankimazin. I can't go to a pharmacy because I don't have a prescription, and honestly, Gabriela, I'm about to explode, I've never felt so bad in my whole life.

—All the more reason. What you need is a good party.

—Honestly, I can't . . .

—Drop by, even if it's only for an hour. Barenboim is determined to get you to direct *The Magic Flute*. Have a little chat with him and you can take some Trankimazin.

—Gabriela, please. —I am begging now.

—Oh, come on, don't be such a drag! —shouts Gabriela.

I have no choice. I'm going up to the party with Beau. Luckily, Gabriela opens the door. I drag her through the kitchen into her bedroom to avoid the living room full of loud, strung-out guests. I finally convince her that I'm in a bad way. I don't usually make this kind of scene, that's *her* specialty. She's completely shameless, I'm a bit more dignified. And she knows it.

Gabriela gives me four 0.5-milligram tabs of Trankimazin, keeping two for herself for tomorrow morning since there still remains lots of coke to snort and tequila to drink. It's astonishing how she manages to keep up this pace at the age of fifty-five.

I put a tab under my tongue and lie down on the bed in her room, a super king-size full of guests' coats, lots of fur. I slide under the pile of coats, only my head is visible. Beau perches as best he can. I tell Gabriela to leave us until the tranquilizer kicks in and promise I'll talk to Barenboim afterward, but only for a moment. She takes her leave. I recognize that she is the perfect hostess, although it's been a long time since I was able to keep up with her.

The Following Day

I wake up feeling better. Beau has to go to his mother's. He wants to make sure that I'm alright. I tell him to do what he needs to do. Besides, I need to be alone to see whether I'm really doing as well as I think.

The minute Beau steps out the door, I feel my cheeks start to burn and the nervous jolts rip through my chest. I don't think about it for a minute. I take another sublingual Trankimazin. I need something to pass the time. And I don't want to take advantage of Beau. I'm seeing him tonight anyway. I quickly scan the cinema show times for a comedy. I settle on Michel Gondry's *Eternal Sunshine of the Spotless Mind*. It starts in half an hour.

In the taxi, I make a few calls, get the name of an on-call psychiatrist. I can see him this evening. Right now, I need something to feed my head. I call Patricia, she asks me how I'm feeling, I tell her about my visit to Gabriela and ask whether I can come see her. She says of course, she'll be at home all day with Lorena, her four-year-old daughter. That should take up the next four hours. I call Beau to tell him everything's fine, and that I'm going to see Gondry's movie.

When the taxi gets to the city center, the streets are teeming with crowds of people. It's like a protest march where every demonstrator has a different slogan and a different cause. Utter chaos. I feel horrendous. The taxi is stuck in traffic. I pay the driver and get out. I run the last stretch to the cinema, pushing my way through the crowd.

Neither Michel Gondry nor his movie is to blame for not distracting me from the successive waves of suffocating panic.

They're less frequent now, but they're still there so I don't mistakenly think that I'm better than I am. I make a mental note of everything I'm feeling so I can tell the psychiatrist. I make it through the entire film. I go out to the Plaza de los Cubos on Calle Princesa.

My first call is to Beau. He's really worried and blaming himself for leaving me on my own. I manage to convince him that I'm fine, that I've seen the movie, that I didn't walk out, which proves that I still have some control over myself.

—Shall I come round to your place? —he says.

—I've arranged some things to fill up the afternoon —I say—, so you'd have a little time with your mother.

Beau almost sounds disappointed and I'm overcome by how much I love him but I don't want him to hear me sounding weak, because I'm already welling up. I tell him that I'm going to Patricia's place and that I'm going to buy something for her daughter at Vips. I tell him I'll see him this evening.

Patricia

Patricia opens the door. We're not just people who work together, we're friends. Sometimes weeks go by without our talking about anything personal. She and I aren't the kind of people to bore their friends to tears. When it comes to confiding in each other, we're more tight-lipped, more masculine.

More to make sure that we're going to be alone than anything, I ask after her husband, the father of her daughter. As I suspected, he's out of town, which is a relief. He works as a sales rep for a brand of American bicycles and is constantly on the road. I know this guy has a second life, maybe even a third, somewhere outside Madrid, or even in Madrid. Patricia knows it too. She's been on the brink of leaving him too many times. It's only in moments like that, when driven by rage, that she confides in me and tells me about all the shit she's had to put up with. Her husband is seriously evil. Since her last attempt at a breakup, which was supposed to be permanent, it's been neither one thing nor the other.

Although we're friends, I don't ask about her problems anymore, and I don't tell her mine, because I don't want to make her uncomfortable. Like I said, we're both pretty macho. Two inhibited people, if they have a good heart, can be soul mates and support each other. Silence gets a lot of bad press, but it's not so bad.

Patricia's eyes are naturally sad, but that afternoon, outside her door, the sadness is immeasurable. I don't ask her anything, I simply give her a look that says I am here for her if she needs me.

Since neither Patricia nor I am particularly talkative, I focus on her daughter, Lo. Lorena. I give her the gifts I've brought. She takes them, but doesn't say a word. She's drawing on a blackboard. I ask her for a kiss and she walks past me, she doesn't even answer. I try to kiss her, but she doesn't let me. The kid doesn't like me, and I find her aversion toward me amusing.

Her mother and I go into the living room and she follows and carries on playing. I spend three-quarters of an hour studying her. Looking at a child is like looking at the sea or into a fire. They are always genuine, and constantly renewed, oblivious to your gaze.

On the television, they're showing *Frida*. Chavela Vargas appears, her hair slicked back. She sings a verse of "La Llorona." It's a version improvised for the movie and I find it disappointing. Chavela's voice trembles and she is slightly out of tune. I mute the sound and say:

—She was already losing her voice by this stage.

I talk nostalgically about the Mexican singer. Patricia looks at me and realizes that I am more sensitive than usual, having spent two nights suffering panic attacks. To say nothing of the hustle and bustle of Christmas.

Thesis on "La Llorona"

—I must have heard Chavela sing "La Llorona" at least fifty times, every one of them different, and I cried every time. In later years, Chavela had lost her voice (but her talent was still there, and all the bitterness and loneliness of rejection. It was all there, in fact it was heightened). Gradually, Chavela began to *speak* the song more and more, and *sing* it less and less. In her last concerts she didn't sing a single line, she would begin by declaiming the lyrics and toward the end she was whispering. The effect was chilling. Hushed as the cloister of a convent, as she used to say. She saved a howl for the end. The last verse begins in a whispered murmur, leading on from the previous murmur: "I want you and yet you, Llorona, you want me to want you more. Already I've given my life, Llorona," she howls, thunderous, defiant, "what more is there to want?" In the final line, the vocal torrent she has held in check in the early verses bursts forth: "YOU WANT MORE!!" At this, the audience always erupts in a roar.

Perhaps the only people who truly get it are those of us who witnessed the miracle.

—I must have the CD somewhere —Patricia says with that gentle apathy of hers.

Bitter Christmas

Without waiting for her to do so, I wander over to the corner where she has her CD player and her CDs and look for one by Chavela. Actually, I'm not really trying to find it, I'm just keeping myself busy after my impromptu speech. I think I need to watch what I say, avoid these flights of fancy where I talk like I'm stoned on drugs. Or maybe I am stoned on the Trankimazin and it's had the opposite effect.

Needless to say, because I'm in no hurry to find it, I stumble on the CD straightaway. I read the track list. "La Llorona," the 1995 version where she first started to *speak* the lyrics. "My Night of Love." "Think About Me." "My Churrasca." "The Simple Things." "Bitter Christmas." Given that it's December,

I decide this last song best fits the occasion. And I put it in the CD player. It's a carol that goes like this:

I loved this cold December now you're leaving
For me, let Christmas be your cruel goodbye
I do not want to start the new year grieving
for love that has so often made me cry.
But there will come a day when you remember
and you are filled with sadness and dismay
you'll understand that in this cruel December
what you loved the most you cast away.
I loved this cold December now you're leaving
For me, let Christmas be your cruel goodbye
I do not want to start the new year grieving
for love that has so often made me cry.

Sitting on the sofa, I listen to the song in silence. From here I can see Patricia is standing in the kitchen. She makes no sound, she does not move, like Anjelica Huston in *The Dead* when she leaves the family party, and as she heads downstairs, she hears a song and stands, frozen, with one hand on the banister.

I can guess the reason for Patricia's stillness. Chavela's lyrics. The song has taken us both by surprise.

Silence. The little girl carries on playing, the song cannot pierce her childish games.

Still, Patricia stands in the kitchen, keeping her back to us, paralyzed by her fear of leaving Lorena's father, at least that's how I see it. And by the fact that this bitter Christmas might be the one where she breaks free.

It is the little girl who breaks the silence, handing me a nut from a large bowl. I try to open it, concentrating on the task as though it is of vital importance. The girl brings over a nut-cracker in the shape of a flat metal heart that works by insert-ing the pointed tip between the two halves of the shell and twisting. I open the first nut. The only sound in the apartment is the dull crack of the shell, and I feel as though it's Patricia who is cracking. Lorena decides that it's easiest to get me to crack the nuts for her, and we launch into an endless cycle where she gives me a nut to crack, and while she's eating it, she hands me another, and so on. I'm just happy to have something to do.

Slowly, Patricia comes back into the living room and sits down on the sofa next to me. Something in her eyes tells me that her heart is brimming with the poison injected in her by the song. She doesn't say anything, she just drinks her beer straight from the bottle. I explain to the little girl which parts of the nut are edible and which aren't. And Patricia just looks at us, broken, and poisoned with hatred.

Epilogue

When I go back downstairs and walk along the street, I real-ize that in all the time I spent with Patricia and her daughter, I didn't have a single panic attack.

This is the first thing I tell the psychiatrist during our initial session shortly afterward. He recommends shock therapy and prescribes Huberplex, which also fails to eradicate the illness.

I sleep with Beau. More than ever, I seek refuge in his body, and I don't know why I have the feeling that, sometime in the future, I'm going to be unfair to him.

I still see a different psychiatrist. I finally got through the hellish long weekend. The first days of my return to normality are the happiest of my life.

ADIÓS, VOLCANO

After twenty years spent searching for her in all her usual haunts, and having finally found her in the tiny back-stage dressing room of the Sala Caracol in Madrid, I have spent another twenty years saying goodbye to her, culminating in this extended farewell, beneath the blistering August sun in Madrid.

Chavela Vargas fashioned loneliness and abandonment into a cathedral that turned no one away and from which we emerged reconciled to our mistakes, and willing to carry on making them—to try again.

In the words of the great Mexican writer Carlos Monsiváis: "Chavela Vargas knew how to convey the desolation of *canciones rancheras* with the radical nakedness of blues." He goes on to say that, by dispensing with the traditional mariachi arrangements, Chavela took away the festive nature of the *rancheras* to expose the stark pain and loss of the lyrics. In "Piensa en mí," a *danzón* by Agustín Lara, Chavela changed the original tempo so drastically, in my opinion, that this lively, danceable song became a *fado* or a mournful lullaby.

No living creature ever sang the brilliant José Alfredo Jiménez with the same heartache as Chavela did. By emphasizing the endings of these songs, Chavela created a new genre that deserves to bear her name. José Alfredo's songs sprang from the margins of society and speak of loss and loneliness. To this, Chavela added a caustic bitterness, superimposing the hypocrisy of the world in which she lived and to which she sang defiantly. She gloried in these endings, transformed a lament into a hymn, then spat the ending in your face. As a member of the audience, I found the experience overwhelming. We're not accustomed to having a mirror held up so closely, the final wave of pain and anguish literally tore me apart. I'm not exaggerating. There must be someone else out there who felt what I did.

In her second act, now in her seventies, time and Chavela went hand in hand. In Spain she found the mutual understanding that Mexico had denied her. And, nurtured by this compassion, Chavela reached a tranquil pinnacle, her songs had a greater gentleness, unfurling all the love that nestled in her repertoire. Throughout the 1990s and into the new millennium, Chavela lived out this endless, joyful night of love with our country, and like every member of the audience, I felt as though she were living her night of love with me alone.

I introduced her onstage in dozens of cities. I remember each and every time, the moments in the dressing rooms before the concert. She had given up alcohol and I'd given up cigarettes, and in those moments, we were like two sets of withdrawal symptoms. She'd tell me she longed for a glass of tequila, to warm up her voice, and I'd tell her that I could literally eat a pack of cigarettes just to ward off my panic, and we'd end up laughing, holding hands, kissing. We kissed a lot, I am intimately familiar with her skin.

The crowning of her career in Spain made it possible for Chavela to make her debut at the Olympia in Paris, something only one other Mexican, the great Lola Beltrán, had done before her. I was sitting in the stalls with Jeanne Moreau beside me. From time to time, I translated a lyric from a song until Moreau whispered, "There's no need, Pedro, I understand her perfectly," and not because she spoke Spanish.

With her dazzling performance at the Paris Olympia, Chavela finally managed to open the doors that, for years, had remained resolutely closed—those of the Palacio de Bellas Artes in Mexico City, another of her dreams. Before the Paris concert, a Mexican journalist thanked me for my generosity toward Chavela. I told him that it was not generosity, but pure selfishness, that I got much more than I gave. I also told him that, although I didn't believe in generosity, I did believe in thanklessness, specifically referring to the country whose culture Chavela most passionately championed. It's true that, from the time she started singing in small clubs back in the

1950s (what I would have given to be at El Alacrán when she made her debut with the exotic dancer Tongolele!), Chavela Vargas was a goddess, but a minor goddess. She told me that she was never allowed to sing on television or in a theater. After the Olympia, her circumstances changed radically.

That night, in the Bellas Artes in Mexico City, I once again had the privilege of introducing her. Chavela had fulfilled another of her dreams and we went out to celebrate, to share it with the person who most deserved it, José Alfredo Jiménez, at Tenampa, a famous bar on the Plaza de Garibaldi. Sitting beneath one of the murals depicting the peerless José Alfredo, we drank and sang until dawn (Chavela drank only water, but the following day, the front pages of the local newspapers ran the headline "Chavela Is Drinking Again"). Those of us lucky enough to be with her that night sang until we were delirious, but it was mostly Chavela who sang, with a mariachi band we had hired for the occasion. It was the first time we heard her accompanied by an original and traditional ensemble. And it was a miracle, one of many that I experienced with her.

On her last visit to Madrid, at an intimate lunch with Elena Benarroch, Mariana Gyalui, and Fernando Iglesias, three days before her performance at the Residencia de Estudiantes, Elena asked Chavela whether she ever forgot the lyrics to her songs. Chavela said, "Sometimes, but I always end up where I should." I could get this sentence tattooed in her honor—how many times had I seen her end up where she should! That night at the incomparable Tenampa, Chavela ended up where she should, beneath the portrait of her beloved drinking buddy José Alfredo, accompanied by a mariachi band. The songs she had made so heartrending in the past accompanied by two guitars, now sounded playful and festive, just as they were meant to be. That night "El último trago" ("The Last Drink") was a glorious hymn to the joys of having drunk life dry, of having loved wantonly, and of still being alive to sing about it. Abandonment was transformed into celebration.

Four years ago, I went to visit the part of Tepoztlán where she lived, at the foot of a hill with the unpronounceable name Chalchitépetl. It was there in those hills and valleys that they had filmed *The Magnificent Seven*, the American version of Kurosawa's *Seven Samurai*. Chavela tells me that, according to legend, when the apocalypse comes, the hill will open its gates and only those who manage to seek shelter in its bosom will be saved. She pointed out the place on the hillside where those very gates seemed to be drawn.

This part of Morelos teems with legends, organic, spiritual, botanical, and sidereal. In addition to the hills, which are more rock than soil, Chavela also lives near a volcano with the thunderous name Popocatépetl—an active volcano, with a past as a human lover, bowed before the lifeless body of his beloved. I note the names as they fall from Chavela's lips and admit I have difficulty pronouncing the final "petl": she tells me that, at one time, women were forbidden from uttering these syllables. Why? Just because they were women, she says. One of the most irrational examples of machismo (all of them are), in a country unashamed of it.

During that visit she also told me, "I'm at peace," and she said it to me again in Madrid. From her lips, the word "peace" takes on its full meaning: she is serene, with no fears, no worries, no expectations (or she has all of these, but that cannot be explained), she is calm. She also said, "One night, I shall stop," and the word "stop" was at once heavy and light, decisive yet casual. "Little by little," she went on, "alone, and I shall enjoy it." This is what she said.

ADIÓS, CHAVELA. Adiós, volcano.

Your husband, in this world, as you liked to call me,

Pedro Almodóvar

REDEMPTION

I am the city jailer and I have borne witness to an event of such magnitude that, for all my lack of skill, I have decided to set it down so that the whole world should know it.

I shall begin at a time before the stranger came to our town, since long before that, rumors had begun to spread about the things he preached in neighboring towns. It was said, and this we were later able to corroborate, that he claimed to be the Messiah, the Son of God, the one for whom we had spent centuries waiting. Inasmuch as it concerns this town, I can say we have never waited for anything or anyone, but after years in which the stranger repeated his claim across the region, we came to be familiar with the utopia of the Messiah.

Utopias are contagious, and they proliferate at a dizzying speed. In this moment, given what I have witnessed, I am no longer completely sure of anything, but I perfectly remember that before he appeared, no one had ever mentioned his name. As is true of all fictions, after the rumors had spread, many people found past evidence of his appearance to corroborate his words, but I firmly believe that this sprang from the imagination of the townspeople. The imagination of a group is greater than that of an individual, however inventive the individual and however dull-witted the members of the group (moreover, I believe that imagination is not related to intelligence). For example, if an individual fires his imagination to create something based on an existing paradigm, and a group does likewise, using the same paradigm, the imaginative capacity of the group will prove considerably greater than that of the individual, and the result will seem more genuine, more consistent.

Perhaps I am mistaken, but personally I attribute the rumors that preceded the stranger's arrival in our town to his self-glorification as he traveled through neighboring towns and villages. By this, I do not mean that his actions were motivated by deceit, but that his words (and he was a master of language) were pregnant, and fertile, lending him a magical aid.

By the time I encountered him, he had already acquired a number of disciples who always traveled with him and who assumed responsibility for visiting nearby towns to talk about him and his powers. Since already he was quite far-famed, I kept a close watch on him from the first day. He was very handsome, but his beauty was so perfect that it did not quite seem human. I can understand why others admired him, I myself was speechless when I first saw him. This was his great weapon, the reason why he had become so popular. Everyone who saw him was irresistibly drawn to him and, following this initial attraction, took an interest in his words, since he constantly talked and smiled, addressing himself to all those present without distinction. But his words were more impenetrable than his beauty, both belonged to a kind of individual that is rare among us. It was easier to admire his beauty, even if we did not understand it, than his wisdom.

Though his words were not comprehensible, we sensed that his meaning was important. He spoke of eternal life, of perfection, shadows, love, and salvation, but in a language that was unfamiliar to us. Perhaps I am too ignorant, I thought, perhaps that is why I cannot understand. I approached other people and asked them to explain his words, but they could not do so either. Despite this lack of understanding, or perhaps because of it, his words were pleasant and fascinating.

Rumors about what he did and said were growing daily. The stranger was indeed a remarkable individual, but many of the stories that circulated were doubtless untrue. When I heard him speak, I was surprised to discover the same love and admiration he projected was reflected in his face. He seemed to find us as wondrous as we found him. He seemed awestruck by our presence, as though we possessed a beauty that he had not suspected.

As for his manner, I can safely say that there was nothing normal about it. At first, he did not sleep or eat. He showed no evidence of physical needs. When he was not speaking but engrossed in his thoughts, he was no longer with us, his image was like an illusion.

The stranger's fame posed no threat to the authorities. The fact that people gradually fashion a myth invariably entails a certain danger, but the outsider, despite the fascination he exerted over people, did not trouble the government, since his words seemed devoid of political meaning. He was a poet who wove dreams of fantastical worlds and ideas, and this, together with his beauty, meant that there would always be people who followed him. But there came a time when his speeches, though they gained little in their clarity, began to include terms that, because they related to a more immediate reality, might be more easily interpreted—whether in the sense that he intended, I do not know. He said, "My kingdom is not of this world." He had already proclaimed himself to be the Son of the God of that kingdom. He promised a better life to those who followed him, and talked of leading out of darkness those who believed in him and forsook the things of this world.

These and many more direct allusions critical of the government provoked a reaction from the President, who, thinking him to be an eccentric revolutionary possessed of qualities that defied analysis, ordered that the stranger be imprisoned and put on trial, so that he would be forced to give an account of his true intentions.

Fear prevented his many supporters from protesting this

injustice. After the surprise of his arrest, there was an entente with the government, because, much as the people admired the stranger, they were as curious as the President to discover whether all the coded messages he had given them were true or false. Once again, the populace revealed their fickle nature.

So, the stranger was imprisoned, and I was his jailer. At that time, the prison housed a famous thief, Barabbas. It fell to the stranger to share a cell with him. I was honored with the responsibility of guarding them both. They were the prisoners who, at that time, aroused the greatest curiosity, and my own was such that, in accordance with my orders, I never left the bars of their cell for an instant.

The stranger had met many people in his public life, but few impressed him as much as Barabbas. The thief lay sprawled at one end of the cell like an animal, filthy and ferocious. With his customary gentleness, the stranger asked:

—Who are you?

Barabbas glared at him, masking his surprise at finding this transcendent individual in his cell.

—What can it matter to you?

—Everything matters to me. I do not think there is anyone whose curiosity could rival mine.

At these eccentric words, Barabbas gave a mocking smile as though determined to have no further conversation with this person he considered a madman. But time spent in the cell is a void that a man will go to any lengths imaginable in order to forget. After a few hours of silence during which the stranger did not trouble him, Barabbas asked:

—What the devil are you doing here?

—I do not know. I have been brought here, but I do not yet understand man well enough to know what it means.

Barabbas smiled contemptuously, then with rising anger, he growled:

—What is this nonsense? Every time you open your mouth you say some foolishness. If you are trying to mock me, then beware.

—On the contrary, I would like to talk about myself, and I would like you to talk to me about yourself, for I must be as strange to you as you are to me.

The stranger said the words with such sincerity that Barabbas's innate loathing of the pedant began to abate.

—I am a thief. They call me Barabbas.

—Why are you a thief?

Barabbas did not know how to interpret the stranger's candor, and after a moment's hesitation, he tried to shrug it off. At first, he had thought this was a madman, but having studied his appearance and his manner he was forced to realize that this was a genuinely sensitive and kindhearted person. Looking at him, he felt even more repugnant. Not only were the stranger's clothes of costly fabrics, but the way he carried himself radiated an aura of perfection and superiority. The thief's boorishness prevented the stranger from noticing the impression his arrival had made. On the other hand, the thief was irritated by his refinement and his manner of speaking. He was not yet convinced that the man was not mocking him, so he said dryly:

—I am a thief because I steal. Or rather, because I have repeatedly been caught stealing.

—And is it wrong to steal? —said the stranger simply.

—What do you think?

—I think they did not reflect before accusing yourself. Who can claim ownership of the things you stole? Besides, when you stole them, you were in need.

—Not always! I have stolen money in order to get drunk, I have stolen from those whose need was greater than mine, and I did so out of sheer wickedness.

Goaded by the rarefied presence of the stranger, Barabbas tried to exaggerate his wickedness, refusing to accept the suggested justifications. In the presence of this man, he felt more despicable than ever and thought it would be grotesque to try to hide his monstrosity. And so he tried to portray himself as more wicked in order to curb his cellmate's compassion.

But the stranger looked at him as though he were a hero.

—You did all that?

—All that and more —said Barabbas—. I am not here on some man's whim. If I were free, the menfolk would fear for their wives and daughters.

The stranger was staring at him, unable to contain his astonishment, spellbound by the brutishness of the thief, so unlike his own radiant gentleness.

—And I have killed —said Barabbas.

—You have killed?

The last seemed to impress the stranger all the more. He was thinking about the arrogance of God the Father, seated on his throne, scorning human beings as among the most imperfect of his creations, and was discovering to his surprise that, on a whim, an insignificant creature like Barabbas could flout God's design.

—Yes —said Barabbas, puzzled by the stranger's reaction—. I can't tell you that I enjoyed it, or that I am the only one, there are many like me.

The stranger looked at him eagerly and Barabbas felt shamed by these looks. In other circumstances, he would have raged, but there was something about the stranger that disarmed him.

—Why do you look at me like that, where do you come from?

—I am not of this world.

—Oh, no? —mocked the thief.

—No.

—What then is your world? —Barabbas asked, amused.

—Mankind cannot know it. I am the Son of God, there are no words in any human tongue to speak of the world of God. It is thence that I come.

Barabbas continued in a sarcastic tone:

—Ah, I see, now I understand why you're amazed. You didn't expect human beings to be like me, did you?

—My Father has never spoken to me of your kind. I do not think He understands you well either.

—And why have you come here?

—I have come to save you.

Hearing this, Barabbas assumed that the stranger was also mocking him and joking and roared with laughter. But despite his merriment, he still did not know what to make of this cellmate. However curious his words, there was something mysterious in the way he spoke that made them ring true. In any event, Barabbas's laughter grew louder, and the stranger, admiring his wild spontaneity, was infected and laughed with him.

I cannot put to words the surprise I felt to hear the two prisoners laughing as though they were old friends.

But for the silence of night, I should not have heard what happened that first night in the cell. The two prisoners jesting like schoolboys until it was late, then silent for a while, unsure what to do or say to one other. I could scarcely see them, but I could imagine the tension of them finding themselves mutually fascinated and thrown together in the solitude of the cell. Each was the prime example of the difference between their worlds. Barabbas was astounded by the beauty and gentleness, the tenderness and eccentricity of the stranger. Meanwhile, the stranger was equally fascinated by the ugliness and brutishness, the suffering and wretchedness of Barabbas. They carried on talking, and shortly afterward I heard them retire. The cell was in utter darkness, but I could just perceive the outlines of their bodies, panting and shuddering, on the same bed.

The following morning, I brought them something to eat. It was the first time I had been in the cell since the stranger arrived. Both were serene. Barabbas's manliness seemed radiant.

The stranger reluctantly accepted food, then as though he had just made up his mind, he said:

—Yes, I wish to do all the things that man has done, I wish to be one of you.

The thief and I both looked at him, realizing that he was indeed no ordinary creature.

Despite the scant hours they had spent together, each had come to terms with their attraction. The frankness of their behavior had effaced the differences between them. They spoke carelessly, confidently.

—So, you have come to save us —said Barabbas—. What think you of this place where you've been brought?

—I have been brought to the finest place. Through you, I am discovering the wonder of what it is to be human.

—So, aside from being the Son of God, which is provocation enough, why have you been imprisoned?

—I do not know. Perhaps, from mankind's point of view, I have committed some crime, but I do not know what it might be.

—And you are not worried?

—No.

—You are heedless. Do you know how close to death we are here in this cell?

—I shall die, so it has been fated, but my death will have a different meaning.

—Please —by now Barabbas had abandoned all boorishness—, if you are jesting, tell me so. You cannot understand the dangers you court by the things you say.

In the presence of the stranger, this most brutal and fearsome rogue no longer recognized himself, concerned as he was for someone other than himself.

—My Father should have told me about man, since He sent me so I could be one of them. He was rash in drawing up a plan concerning something He does not truly understand. Since I came into your world, I have constantly felt alien, thus have I been brooding on my own essence, oblivious to man. But since yesterday, when I stepped into this cell, I have begun to discover what man is, and taken an interest in his plight. Now, knowing more about you, I feel more human.

—If what you say is true, then go no further. Do not descend to the depths of misery. Look on me, behold the wretch you might become.

—How can you say this? Human beings are a different kind of divinity.

—Cease your babble! —Barabbas was angered by the stranger's senselessness—. Divinity, I warrant, is possessed of certain qualities?

—Man, too, possesses them.

—We? What you say is folly.

—You experience a great variety of emotions. I am beginning

to feel human because I too have begun to feel. In my kind, harmony is not pleasure, it is nothing. I feel nothing for my Father, and He, nothing for me. For us, past, present, and future are equal and immutable. We live as in a tranquil and unvarying dream. Man feels hate, fear, love. Last night, I felt I understood passion, and there is nothing to which I can compare it. Now, I feel melancholy, I do not know why, but I would like to weep, and for this, too, I have nothing to compare.

—Well, we know. Hate is not good, nor is fear, nor love. Such things are terrible.

—I have no means to compare what is terrible. Your existence is all of these things at once, ours is the absence of such things.

—Here with me, you shall have time to discover many other facets. You could not have chosen a worse exemplar, we shall see whether you continue to find us so admirable.

—I need no more time to be convinced. Your vital spirit, the vital spirit of all men, do you understand what it means? You are capable of destruction . . .

—Destruction, me?

—You said as much yourself. You have killed, have you not?

—Yes, but I have also been a victim.

—To kill is to defy the laws of God, my Father.

—And He, your Almighty Father, does He not destroy?

—My Father is a continuous unconsciousness. He can neither create nor destroy. He has sent me so that, with your influence, the future of our kingdom will be changed.

—Your Father is as mad as you.

—I am glad to be here —said the stranger after a brief pause.

AT FIRST, AS I have said, Barabbas and the stranger were antithetical. I suppose this is what captivated each from the first moment. On the third day, when I gave them their food, both had changed. Barabbas was no longer such a brute, and the stranger seemed less perfect and less noble than before. Over time, their mutual influence increased. The stranger, doing his Father's bidding, had become a true man: he experienced hunger and he experienced love, he felt as cold and dirty as any man who had languished in prison for three days. Yet he was happy to have achieved this. He had forgotten who he was, until called upon to face the judge and the people. Now, he remembered his mission. The hardest part was yet to come, and now that he was finally a man, he felt restricted and afraid.

The people expected a thrilling clash between the authorities and the curious stranger, and whatever the outcome, the spectacle promised to be dazzling. In their hearts they had accepted the President's unfairness as a test of the powers of the stranger.

But the stranger did not appear alone. Barabbas was also present at the trial, unaware of the part he was to play.

The first anticlimax came when the stranger appeared. He

looked filthy and tired, his face bore the signs of suspicion and mistrust, gone was the power to persuade that only days before he radiated without the need to say a single word. Seeing him so human, so vulnerable, the people began to turn against him. Faced with this first impression, the myth he represented for those who knew him crumbled. Having seen him, many began to despise him. Others, including his closest disciples, impatiently waited for him to say the first word and dispel their fears. But the stranger, having been defeated, stood with his head bowed and waited to be asked a question, as though he had nothing to say.

The Prosecutor began:

—You are accused of claiming that you are the Son of God, and that your kingdom is not of this world, but another. Is this true?

The stranger, confused and ashamed by his pretentious words, could only nod, since he remembered having said these things, but dared not speak. The people began to hurl insults, they felt cheated by all that had been mere façade before he was arrested.

—Answer the question. Is this true? —the Prosecutor insisted—. Has your memory failed, or is it that you cannot speak?

With great effort, the stranger said:

—Yes, it is true.

The people laughed at his fears, and even his closest disciples denied ever having known him.

—Is it true that you have promised that whosoever shall

follow you will have a better life? —the Prosecutor relentlessly continued—. Is it true that, in order for them to get the things you promise, they must forsake everything, including their parents, their lands, and their friends?

The stranger considered a moment, *How could I have said such things?* But he knew that the Prosecutor was not lying, he had often spoken thus. How far he was now from such grandiloquence!

—God, Father! —he muttered, filled with fear. And, indifferent to his circumstance, God the Father answered from within him: *Do not fear. You know all this is mere formality, this too shall pass. You are doing very well.*

But . . . the stranger tried to protest.

But you have lost confidence in me, God grumbled.

Interrupting these thoughts, and trying to calm the people's jeers, the Prosecutor roared:

—Give me your answer, is it true or false?

Ashamed and remorseful, the stranger murmured:

—It is true.

Another shower of insults. Barabbas stared angrily at the people. He was suffering as much as his friend, but there was nothing he could do.

—Tell me, then, how you dare say such things? Your words are a threat to the good of the nation. You promise fantasies to those who heed your words, you sow turmoil and dissent among the people. Who are you that you should promise an end to poverty, disease, depravity, and injustice?

—The Son of God? —came the deafening chorus of those supporting the Prosecutor.

—Who do you hope to convince of such madness? Have you but seen yourself? Even a beggar would not look so wretched, even Barabbas himself.

At this, all eyes turned to the thief, the mob shouted and jeered.

—Look on him, does not Barabbas look more like the Son of God than this miserable wretch?

The Prosecutor pandered to the people, and they laughed in amusement, as though intent only on showing their wit.

—But despite the insignificance of your boasts, you have committed the serious crime of disturbing the peace and affronting the authorities, and this warrants punishment.

The President watched the scene with disgust, exasperated that he was expected to intervene in such a tenuous matter.

—Come, come, Mr. Prosecutor —he said—, do not vex yourself, it is not worth it. Many a madman has said worse.

—An example needs to be set so that, in future, such men will be careful about what they say in public.

—Very well. Then I shall leave you, I have had my fill. Do with him as you see fit. I entrust to you the responsibility of the verdict.

The Prosecutor, spurred on by the hoi polloi, and unfettered by the presence of the President, had the idea of flattering the assembled company by leaving the nature of the sentence to them. The crimes of Barabbas were known to

all, and the next day he was to be crucified, yet in that moment Barabbas elicited more sympathy than the misbegotten
stranger. The public Prosecutor left it to the people to decide
which of the two should live, and the people, in a thunderous
clamor, chose Barabbas.

The stranger was glad to have saved the thief's life, but
wept with fear at the thought of his own death. At no time
did the thought of future resurrection and ascension to
heaven give him succor. He did not even think of it. Being a
man, his sole passion was for mankind, and from them came
his only fear.

BARABBAS WAS RELEASED and the stranger taken back to
his cell. That night, he could know the depths of human suffering, if he truly was the Son of God. On that endless night,
the agony of his impending death was made greater by the
absence of the thief. The one thing that sustained him was
the thought that Barabbas had been redeemed, even if the
thought of being separated from him was intolerable.

The populace joyfully embraced the new Barabbas. Pros-
titutes offered him their bodies bathed in wine and were surprised when Barabbas refused. He roamed the city, a stranger
to himself and what, till then, had been his home. For him
too, this was a night of agony, I am told. To every greeting
he responded with a roar, and some regretted having saved
him. He considered fleeing, but the thought of abandoning

the stranger stopped him from taking the first step. He went to the prison and, from what the sentries told me, prowled about till dawn.

The following day the stranger was taken and led to the mountain where he was to be crucified. The cross had been brought to the prison so he could carry it to the place of execution. Never have I seen anyone look so helpless.

When we emerged, Barabbas was there, like a dog without a master. The stranger did not see him, since the weight of the wood bowed his head and forced him to look down at the ground.

With extraordinary humility, Barabbas asked the guards if he might help the stranger carry the piece of wood. The surprised guards granted their permission. Only then did the former Son of God become aware of his friend's presence.

—What are you doing? —he asked wearily.

—Going with you.

—Go, make the most of your freedom. The true meaning of my death is that you may live. Go before they change their minds.

—I have nothing to do.

—Carry on stealing, killing, raping. Abuse your power.

—Last night I discovered that there is nothing that I want to do, that I no longer want to do the things that interested me. You have changed me.

—Do not talk so. Do not make a senseless sacrifice more difficult.

—You need not worry, you have your mission to fulfill.

—No, now I fear death. I care nothing for my mission, I can think only about me, about you.

—But what of your Father?

—I do not know, He is far from here, I can no longer feel Him.

—I didn't dare suggest it, but if you no longer care about your mission, why not forsake all this and flee?

—Flee?

—Yes.

—I do not have the strength to stand upright.

—Leave that to me.

Without giving them time to react, Barabbas grabbed the cross and swung it at the guards. Then, having knocked them to the ground, he took the stranger in his arms and fled into the mountains.

MEMORY OF AN EMPTY DAY

Maundy Thursday. Bright sunshine streaming through the window, but I can't think what to do with the day that stretches out before me. Is it entertaining or interesting to write about a tedious and boring day? I dread such days.

I've finished watching the Ryan Murphy series about Andy Warhol's diaries. There wasn't much left to watch. It's rare for me to watch TV in the morning, but today is a special day.

When Warhol came to Madrid, I was invited to all the parties in his honor. It was 1983, and he had come to promote his exhibition of guns, crucifixes, and knives. Over and over at every party, we were introduced and he never said a single word to me. His way of reacting was to sometimes take a photo of you with a little camera that he always carried.

Everyone who introduced me said the same thing: this man (meaning me) is the Spanish Warhol. The fifth time they said this, he asked me why people called me the Spanish Warhol, and feeling deeply embarrassed, I said, "I suppose because I make movies starring transvestites and transsexuals." An excruciating encounter. Essentially, he had come to Spain so the millionaires who appear in *¡Hola!* magazine could commission a portrait. All the parties were at the homes of snobby millionaires, noblemen and bankers, but not one commissioned anything. I would have asked him for a portrait, but in those days, I didn't have the money.

The thing I most liked about the TV series were the images documenting Warhol's relationship with Basquiat: theirs was a true love story without the sex. It's obvious how much Basquiat worshiped and respected Warhol, who at some point became his mentor. When they decided to work together, they made about two hundred paintings. I saw them at a Paris exhibition and I loved them. Warhol himself says that Basquiat is the better painter. And I agree.

I am also interested in the moment when their joint work was presented in New York, a major event for the art world: the critics were lukewarm and dismissive. They said that Basquiat was simply Warhol's pet. These days, no one doubts his talent, but I think the New York critics of the time were spiteful and cruel. And that it probably put them off the extraordinary experience of working together.

I'm surprised that both artists were so sensitive to what

people wrote about them, I assumed that they were above such things.

I'm surprised by the constant references to Warhol's homosexuality and his entourage, I'm surprised to find more than one critic or specialist talking about Warhol's longing to be accepted as a gay artist and about the mask he conscientiously constructed (with considerable talent) to leave the person he truly was at home and appear as an almost grotesque character he had created in plain sight. Without managing to fool anyone. I can understand that such things might have amused him for a while, that you just want to be the most banal avatar of yourself with the world, but to spend your whole life like that?

I had thought that, with Warhol living in the most tolerant city in the world, in an avant-garde artistic environment, it wouldn't occur to anyone to wonder whether he was gay or straight. Just as it would never occur to the second great love of his life, an executive at Paramount, to ever admit it. But, come to think of it, in the mid-1980s I suppose that openly expressing your homosexuality was like saying you had a bomb in your pocket that could explode at any moment.

I suspect that when they were filming *Heat*, *Flesh*, or *Trash* (Paul Morrissey in the shadow of Warhol), nobody thought about it at all, any more than they did with Warhol's own early films, *Sleep*, *Lonesome Cowboys*, *Chelsea Girls*, or *Women in Revolt*. How naive of me! When looking at the life and work of Warhol or Basquiat, it never occurred to me to think about their sexuality or the color of Basquiat's skin, but according to the documentary, many people obsess about such details.

I HAVE TO admit that when they were first published, I bought Warhol's diaries and started reading them, but only got through the first few pages. All he wrote about, at least at the start, were taxi rides and exactly how much they had cost. I didn't have the patience to carry on.

This is the first time I've written about the "present," by which I mean I'm trying to keep a diary of the times I live in (well, sometimes I take notes on my promotional tours; and when my mother died, I wanted to set down exactly how I felt the next morning, I wanted to remember it in detail). I usually find writing about myself boring, but I'm fascinated by writers or artists talking or writing about themselves. In this sense I find it curious that Andy's *Diaries* weren't written by him, that every morning, when he woke up, he called Pat Hackett and, over the phone, recounted everything he had done the previous day (not to mention the price of everything: I think this is the subject of his literary work, noting the price of everything, even if it's just a taxi fare). If you decide to keep a record of your life, including the minute details, I think the pleasure lies in personally collating them and putting them into words. To me, that's the game of reflecting or being reflected on the page as though it were a mirror. I wonder whether Warhol ever read the *Diaries* after they were edited. I suspect he didn't. Despite the fact it's about his life, I can't imagine him reading a thousand-page doorstop.

I ARRIVED IN this New York five years too late, at the height of the AIDS crisis. People were living with the pandemic that had taken the most important artists of that time and of that city. I was there for the release of *Tie Me Up! Tie Me Down!* following the huge success of *Women on the Verge of a Nervous Breakdown.*

New York is a city of continual reinvention, a city that knows how to rise again from its tragedies. I missed the wild nights at Studio 54, but when I was there, in 1990, New York nights had lost none of their wildness, their glamour or charm. A different era had been born, but New York was still New York. The greatest extravaganzas were hosted by drag queens, with RuPaul and Lady Bunny leading the charge. In record time, they had established themselves as the queens of New York nightlife, along with Susanne Bartsch, a woman, but as dragtastic as the rest. All three knew how to bring a spark of joy to a city devastated by grief and loss.

I remember having gypsy dresses run up in Spain, which I used to dress RuPaul and Lady Bunny, who were hosting the New York premiere of *Tie Me Up! Tie Me Down!* together with Liza Minnelli, who agreed to sing "New York, New York" to me as she descended the metal staircase of the recently opened club the Sound Factory, a converted warehouse. As we walked to the staircase, I noticed she was shaking (she had just come out of rehab and was still fragile). She said: "You just tell me what you want me to do. I'm the daughter of a film director, you know."

Life carried on, and there were new kinds of celebration to make up for the fact I had not been there ten years earlier. It was the time when the *houses* were holding their dazzling *balls* in the fashionable clubs. I witnessed the very beginnings of voguing, before the documentary *Paris Is Burning* and Madonna's "Vogue," and three decades before the TV series *Pose*.

BEFORE I FORGET—especially since I'm talking about the King of Pop Art—I'd like to mention the greatest example of pop art I've seen recently. I was channel surfing when suddenly, on some magazine show, I saw this tattoo artist appear who had created a design based on the Will Smith–slapping–Chris Rock incident. He shows off the drawing—it's two dimensional, a simple line drawing, but very precise. He also shows the leg of the first client to get the tattoo.

Writing as I am doing now reminds me of a book I read on the last flight to Los Angeles (to attend the Oscars), by Leïla Slimani, an author whose novel *The Perfect Nanny* (winner of the Prix Goncourt in 2016) I had adored. I hunt it out and flick through it again, it's called *The Scent of Flowers at Night*. You get the impression that this is a book she is writing because she feels she has to, and she starts by talking about needing isolation in order to be able to focus on writing. In her words, "seclusion seems to me the one condition necessary for Life to happen. As if, by separating myself from the noise of the world, by protecting myself, another world might emerge from within me." I picture her alone in the place where she writes, not answering the phone, rejecting all contact with the outside world, sitting in front of her computer, waiting for an idea to come, or simply writing about that tension: the emptiness of barren days. Her emptiness, if you can call it that, is different from mine.

I have come to this place of almost total isolation as a result of not replying to others, of not having worked on genuine friendships or neglecting the ones I had. My solitude is the result of never having cared about anyone except myself. And little by little people disappear. On days like today, my loneliness is a terrible burden, it doesn't matter that I'm accustomed to it, that I'm an expert loner. I don't like it, and it often distresses me. That's why I need to be constantly involved in working on a film, but although that's fine right now, with three projects lined up, there are always holidays, there's bloody Holy Week, when all activity grinds to a halt because people in my office are off, and my brother and the few friends I have leave Madrid.

I SHAKE OFF my boredom, get dressed, and go out into the street. Madrid is empty, except for the pavement opposite where I live and walk, the Paseo de Pintor Rosales, where there are a lot of people lounging on café terraces or strolling around, families with children. On a bench I see a Latin American couple, engaged or recently married, they are both very short and are looking excitedly at the passersby. I also see a lesbian couple, almost identical in their neutral dress style, their casually masculine hairstyles. They're also quite short. They are older. I'd love to know more about them. I'm glad that they have found each other. I am always impressed by the silence of couples.

I walk for half an hour, 3,426 steps, 1.59 miles. I really should walk more, but I'm really not able. Just half an hour of necessary walking, and even that is painful, especially in the lumbar region, since the surgery on my back.

"TO WRITE, YOU must refuse yourself to others; refuse them your presence, your love. You must disappoint your friends and your children. For me, this discipline is a source of satisfaction, even happiness, and at the same time, the cause of my melancholy," Slimani says in her book. I don't agree, or not entirely. I've taken this paragraph literally and it's brought me no happiness or satisfaction, but lots of melancholy. It's unpleasant, at least to me, to realize that you're begrudging with your time, even if the business of writing and directing films is one that completely absorbs you. Maybe Leïla Slimani is right that her work and mine require countless hours of isolation, but I deeply miss the contact with other people's lives, and it's difficult to go back to how things were, to a time when I was a social creature and led a more communal life, because as you get older, not everything works in your favor, it's not enough to meet people. Picking up the phone and randomly calling the usual friends isn't always an incentive. And I think that's very detrimental, especially for someone like me, who has fed on everything going on around me to write my screenplays—my mother, my childhood, my time with the priests in Catholic school, my years as a young adult in Madrid, the countless friends I hung out with during La Movida, the conversations overheard, the weirdness of some of those friendships, the pain that was caused by intimate personal relationships. If there was one thing I knew for certain when I was young, it was that I'd never be bored. Now I am bored. And that is a kind of defeat.

I continue reading Slimani, she will serve me as a guide to do something that she did in this book I love, *The Scent of Flowers at Night*. She accepted an invitation from her publisher to spend a whole night locked in a museum. The project was called Ma nuit au musée, and what her editor suggested was that she sleep in the Punta della Dogana, a legendary building in Venice, a former customs house, now a contemporary art gallery, and write about it.

Slimani confesses that she doesn't have much to say about contemporary art, that it doesn't really interest her, but was persuaded by the idea of being shut in, which is why she took up the suggestion. In her book—like me in this moment, but with much greater talent and more interesting things to relate—Slimani allows herself to be swept away by these works exhibited for her eyes only, which, though she does not always understand them, trigger some internal mechanism that takes her back to her childhood in Rabat, to the true meaning of writing, to her father, and to the twin cultures of Morocco and France to which she belongs, without ever feeling completely French or completely Moroccan, as though straddling two chairs, with one buttock on each.

She also writes about Notre Dame in flames and the suicide of cities, like Venice, where she has to travel so she can spend a night locked in the museum. I am moved when she suggests that Notre Dame took her own life, exhausted at being turned into a tourist attraction to be consumed.

"Being alone in a place that nobody else could enter, a place from which I couldn't escape: it's a writer's fantasy. All of us have these cloistered dreams, visions of a room of our own where we would be both prisoner and guard." Even the idea is something I find terrifying. Perhaps because I am not a novelist, or simply because I suffer from terrible claustrophobia. The book is fascinating and I read it in one sitting. There are underlined passages on every page, but, as I said, I don't agree with many of the ideas expressed by Slimani. And I take a curious pleasure in that.

At one point she writes about how one has to accept one's fate, whether good or bad. I refuse to accept mine and constantly strive to improve it, even if seclusion and stillness are not exactly the best ways to improve anything. But everyone has to make peace with their contradictions. And those I do accept.

For Muslims, Slimani writes a little later, life down here is mere vanity, we are nothing and live at the mercy of Allah. Harsh words for an atheist like me. I do not accept, as she claims, that man's presence in this world is ephemeral and one should not get too attached to it. While it's unarguable that life is ephemeral, it's the only thing to which we can become attached. Instinctively, we search for reasons, for explanations, we are thinking beings.

Men find it hard to accept the cruelty of fate, Slimani writes. And in this case, I think she's talking about me.

Although writing, whether a novel or a screenplay, necessarily demands a lot of time for concentration and solitude, this sense of flow (which you feel once you have settled into the story you want to tell) doesn't always happen when you're sitting in front of a computer. I find it useful to move around a lot. To take a walk, for instance. If I get up from my writing and go for a stroll, my brain carries on writing while I'm walking. In fact, I was out for a walk one day and someone came over and said something, and in a moment of extravagant cheekiness, I said apologetically, "Excuse me, but I'm in the middle of writing." It might sound like a wisecrack, but it was true. When I'm walking, I come up with new ideas to develop the story I'm working on. It also happens on car journeys. And obviously, on long flights. With no reference points to time and space, my ability to focus is increased. Everything I read feeds and inspires me. A lot of the plots for my films, or ideas that overcame a temporary writer's block, have come to me while I've been on a plane, surrounded by sleeping strangers.

I like writers who talk about the act of writing and constantly quote from other authors. Slimani's book is full of reflections about writing. "I don't think writers write to gain relief," she says. I agree. "A writer has an unhealthy attachment to their sufferings, their nightmares. Nothing would be more terrible than being cured of this attachment." I'm not sure. It's true that you don't write when you're happy, or write about happy characters. Tension and conflict are like beats in music, they are indispensable, they give the story a sort of framework, a structure and a rhythm.

IT'S MAUNDY THURSDAY, I haven't turned the TV on all day, but through the windows comes the sound of drums from the religious processions, the smell of burning candles, and the frenzied cries of the faithful (fueled as much by alcohol as faith) as they roam, calling out to the different Virgins in Spanish towns and cities. I can also hear Russian bombs devastating Ukrainian cities. For them there is no truce. The horrors of war allow for no respite, not even during Easter.

And by this point, night has come and I stop writing.

A BAD NOVEL

I've always dreamed of writing a bad novel. Early on, when I was young, my dream was to become a writer, to write a great novel. Over time, reality proved that what I wrote inevitably became a movie, initially Super 8 shorts and later feature films that played in cinemas and were successful. I realized that my writings were not literary stories, but rough drafts of screenplays.

On the face of it, it seems logical that someone who can write a good screenplay could (is destined to) write a good novel. I thought it was just a matter of time, of maturity, of accumulating experiences, of possessing a certain talent, an original eye, a distinctive world, but although I believed I had all these things, I felt as though I was deluding myself. Writing a good screenplay isn't easy, it takes time, hours of seclusion (and narrative skill), and being a little ruthless with yourself, but none of these things makes a good screenplay a novel. No one is stupid enough to think that writing a good screenplay means you're likely to write a good, let alone a great, novel. But it's a legitimate and a human ambition, one you have to guard against, which is why it's important not to fall in love with your own work.

I think this is a weakness I've overcome, or at least gotten firmly under control. The one piece of advice I'd give to all mediocre—and not so mediocre—writers, and one I impose on myself, is an exercise in self-criticism. Self-criticism gives you something of inestimable value: calmness, knowing how to wait. And I waited (I've been waiting now for more than forty years). One of the other positive aspects of self-criticism is that it makes the inevitable disappointment more bearable.

There exists a subgenre known as the novelization. Novels have been adapted from the scripts of various television series and, as it happens, by at least one celebrated writer, Quentin Tarantino, who, immediately after the release of his last film, *Once Upon a Time in Hollywood*, published a novel with the same title and the same characters. I don't know whether he wrote it before or after making the film. I think he started writing the novel and, after a few chapters, decided it should be a film, and wrote the screenplay, which was nominated for a Best Original Screenplay Oscar that was eventually won by *Parasite*, a brilliant film, but one whose screenplay is problematic unless you're addicted to constant plot twists and mutations. There comes a point in a movie at which the plot and the genre have been established and shouldn't change. (I say this, but constantly mix genres. I am very keen on mixing, but not on mutations. This is something I learned with *Kika*, where the mutant mixture proved fatal.) I don't like to be categorical, but I think the third act of *Parasite* is a different film. Maybe I'm letting myself get carried away, because I love both films and both writers. Anyway, I was talking about the screenplay-turned-novel. There are many less illustrious examples than the two I have just mentioned.

In most cases, novelization is a means of spinning out the success of the movie by repackaging it as a novel, and I'm sure they have a readership. Actually, I love the fact that they have their own readership. For a long time, I've adored substitutes, not just in culture, but in food, in fashion, etc. There is a touching innocence to having the desire but not the ability.

But, leaving aside the eventual reader and thinking simply about the author, a novelization is an act of self-delusion, even in autofiction. What is the difference between a screenplay and a novel? One is a story whose primary tool is the word, while the other derives its impact from images without dispensing with the word, which is why some screenplays are described as being literary, because the characters speak a lot. Éric Rohmer is a good example. Ingmar Bergman is even better. I think some of his screenplays were turned into novels, or were published in book form, I don't know whether this was before or after the films. But maybe Bergman, given his roots in theater, is one of the few directors whose screenplays are worth turning into novels, as long as he is the one to write them.

I have to confess that the first sentence in this piece isn't completely true, but I couldn't bear to cut it. I did not always dream of writing a bad novel. It has taken me a long time and quite a few films to admit that, as a novelist, I wouldn't be up to the task, despite the fact that my screenplays are becoming more and more literary and some of my works, had I had the talent, would have made better novels than films, since there is a lot of material that, for reasons of pacing and cinematic calligraphy, doesn't get used in the film. For all the stories I've told, for all the characters I've created (I mean the good ones, not the ones that didn't work), I wrote almost twice as much material as ended up in the film. I have vastly more information about the characters and their stories than appears onscreen. All this additional information could have found its place if I had been writing a novel.

Nothing could be more different from a novelist than a director/screenwriter. The director is a man of action and has to be ruthless in cutting out dialogue, reactions, scenes, sometimes whole characters—because the director is a slave to the story he needs to tell, and to do this he has to field hundreds of questions (I'm not exaggerating) from the cast and crew. He never has enough time, and while the commute may be short, if the movie is being shot in a studio, it is endlessly repeated. If you have a pet, you can't bring it with you. The job of the novelist, on the other hand, is sedentary. You can spend as many hours as you like in front of the computer, you can go for a walk if you feel like it. You don't have to talk to anyone, let alone answer questions during the writing process. You can have cats, and you can stroke them. And drink booze. And chain-smoke. The novelist is free, and though his life may be touched by tragedy, a novelist will always know how to channel it into his art.

But, to return to the question of what distinguishes a screenplay and a novel, I can think of several answers. They are utterly different disciplines. It's not surprising that few great novels ended up being turned into great films. Even Kubrick could not manage it with Nabokov's *Lolita*. Obviously, there are exceptions—*The Dead* by James Joyce/John Huston, or *The Leopard* by Lampedusa/Visconti.

Let me give an example. In a screenplay, you have a character who is going to open the door. Someone has just knocked. In the screenplay you have to describe only the action, that is, So-and-so opens the door. In a novel, during that short journey (while someone is walking to the door), you can recount the character's whole story and his or her relationship to the world. You can tell everything.

In cinema, there is no such thing as an inner voice, all you can have is voiceover or a flashback, but these do not compare. Both are narrative devices to be handled with great care, unless your name happens to be Martin Scorsese, who specializes in using flashbacks magnificently supported by voiceover.

There came a time, some years ago, when I gave up my dreams of being a novelist, but reading Enrique Vila-Matas's novel *Mac's Problem*, in which the protagonist decides to rewrite an existing novel, *Walter's Problem*, expanded the possibilities of the kind of novel I could write with my limited talent.

Mac is fascinated by posthumously published books and dreams that his novel could appear to be both posthumous and unfinished. He is also fascinated by the idea of being "a falsifier," but I believe that if there's no self-deception, there's no forgery. The important thing is not to deceive yourself (I am suddenly having doubts about that last sentence) and Mac doesn't deceive himself. His plan is to write every day, to fill the empty hours because the day is too long and he has no job to go to anymore. But it's not the discipline of writing a diary that appeals to him, but writing a work of fiction, and for that he needs ideas. He comes across *Walter's Problem*, a novel no one remembers that was savaged when first published, whose author happens to be a neighbor who is rude to him, so he does not feel he owes the man much respect. This constellation of circumstances is enough for Mac to decide to rewrite *Walter's Problem* and, obviously, improve on it. He's not worried about the future, in either legal or literary terms. Maybe he dies before finishing the novel and it becomes a fake posthumous book.

Vila-Matas's hilarious and ingenious novel led me to the conclusion that there are certain people, including me, who feel the need to write a novel, and the quality of that novel should not be a problem, my problem. If I don't think I'm capable of writing a great novel, I could try my hand at another kind of novel whose standing does not depend on its quality and its greatness. It occurred to me that, at the end of the day, a bad novel is a novel, and that, if I forget about the quality, or just stop worrying about it, a bad novel is something I could write. It would be an honest, adult novel, in which the author is completely aware of what he's doing and has transcended his juvenile notions of greatness. It might even be entertaining, it wouldn't be the first.

In Emmanuel Carrère's book *Yoga*, I found a piece of advice that borrows from a book he loves, Carl Seelig's *Walks with Walser*. It is advice for impatient writers: "Take a few sheets of paper and for three days on end write down, without fabrication or hypocrisy, everything that comes into your head. Write down what you think of yourself, of your wife, of the Turkish War, of Goethe, of Fonk's trial, of the Last Judgement, of your superiors—and when three days have passed you will be quite out of your senses with astonishment at the new and unheard-of thoughts you have had. This is the art of becoming an original writer in three days."

I am completely fascinated and in total agreement, but I don't feel capable of carrying out this brilliant exercise. I can write for three days about anything that crosses my mind, without fabrication or hypocrisy. It's something I think I've already done. I don't know whether for three days straight, but certainly for two, over Christmas or Holy Week, the times when loneliness and boredom are worst. It seems more attainable to me than letting my thoughts flow, the way they do in yogic meditation. My mind is constantly invaded by thoughts and songs that insist on keeping me company when I'm silent, which is most of the day if I'm not on set. Mostly songs. Sometimes it's the same song endlessly repeated, until my frantic brain, on my orders, substitutes a different song, which in turn plays on loop, and so on until I fall asleep. It's torture.

I don't mind writing about myself. In fact I'd say it's pretty much the only thing I do. Writing "my women" or "my men" is something I find more difficult—I don't like to include other people in my writing, not unless I've fictionalized them to such an extent that the original inspiration is unrecognizable.

As for the Turkish War and Goethe, I'm afraid I'd have to do a lot of research and I'm not particularly keen on the idea. Besides, it would take me more than three days. As for Fonk's trial, I suppose I could write about any of the crimes that crop up daily in the papers. My superiors? I have no superiors. I'm my own boss.

It's a pity, because Carl Seelig's advice is great, but at the same time it highlights my own limitations and probably those of many aspiring great writers.

Given that I can't, and that I'm too lazy to research the Turkish War, Fonk's trial, and Goethe, I'll look for subjects and characters closer to home. This might be a good start: "I was born in the early 1950s, a terrible period for the people of Spain, but a glorious time for cinema and fashion."

A NOTE FROM THE TRANSLATOR

It is strange to find yourself inside the mind of someone you have known for most of your life yet never met.

Pedro Almodóvar has been a crucial support and influence since my adolescence. His films, which I first discovered in my late teens, offered kaleidoscopic glimpses of a world that was wild, chaotic, and impossibly free. To a young gay man who had grown up in what was still very much Holy Catholic Ireland, Almodóvar's portraits of LGBT lives as complex, individual, and sometimes shimmeringly erotic were truly revolutionary and gloriously life-affirming.

Even his early films—whose transgressive hedonism embraced fetishistic matadors, transvestite hookers, pregnant nuns, and querulous lesbians—were somehow rooted in what it means to be human. More than any living director, he embodies Terence's maxim: "I am human, I consider nothing human alien to me."

When I first read these stories, it felt like taking a journey through my own life. In early stories, I recognized the seeds of some of the films I had found so exhilarating, and I was reminded of people I had loved and places I had lived; in others I rediscovered the extraordinary empathy and humanity that makes Almodóvar's later work so heart-wrenching.

As I read, I discovered a writer with a fierce, ungovernable imagination—something that came as no surprise—and I also became keenly aware of the challenges awaiting me. The stories and *crónicas* in this volume span more than half a century. More than that, they explore very different genres, starkly contrasting registers, and shift effortlessly from comic to gothic, from the plangent to the numinous.

The act of translation is always and ever about voice, about capturing the rhythms and cadences of a text and striving to re-create them. Translators, much like actors, are performers; they seek to inhabit a text the better to make it live in their own language. If working on *The Last Dream* was sometimes challenging, it was also thrilling and deeply satisfying. I can only hope that I have done it justice.

—Frank Wynne

ABOUT THE AUTHOR

Pedro Almodóvar was born in the heart of La Mancha in the 1950s. As a teenager, he left his small town for Madrid to realize his dreams of becoming a filmmaker. Arriving with few prospects and with the National Film School recently shuttered by the dictator Francisco Franco, Almodóvar secured "proper" employment at the National Telephone Company of Spain, which allowed him to purchase his first Super 8 camera. For the next twelve years, Almodóvar split his time between this day job—which gave him unique access and insight into the interior lives and dramas of the Spanish middle class—and nights collaborating with theater groups and punk bands, writing for underground magazines, and making Super 8 films with his friends. This personal renaissance coincided with the explosion of the democratic Madrid, a period known as La Movida. In 1980, after a year and a half of filming on a shoestring budget, Almodóvar made his feature-length debut with *Pepi, Luci, Bom and Other Girls Like Mom*. Since then, he has never stopped writing and directing films, which include the Academy Award–winners *All About My Mother* and *Talk to Her*.

In 1986, he cofounded the production company El Deseo with his brother Agustín. El Deseo has since produced all of Almodóvar's films as well as helped nurture the careers of many talents, not least of which include Guillermo del Toro, Lucrecia Martel, Damián Szifrón, and Isabel Coixet.

The recipient of numerous accolades and distinctions, Almodóvar has been inducted into the French Legion of Honor, awarded the Prince of Asturias Award for the Arts, and received honorary doctorates from both Harvard University and the University of Oxford. He has also won the Venice Film Festival's prestigious Golden Lion as well as two Academy Awards, five BAFTA Film Awards, and two Golden Globes Awards among others.

Here ends Pedro Almodóvar's
The Last Dream.

The first edition of this book was printed
and bound at Lakeside Book Company
in Harrisonburg, Virginia, in August 2024.

A NOTE ON THE TYPE

The text of this novel was set in Sabon, an old-style serif typeface created by Jan Tschichold between 1964 and 1967. He drew inspiration for it from the elegant and highly legible designs of the famed sixteenth-century Parisian typographer and publisher Claude Garamond and named it after Jacques Sabon, one of Garamond's close collaborators. Sabon has remained a popular typeface in book design for its quintessential smooth and clean look.

HARPERVIA

An imprint dedicated to publishing international voices,
offering readers a chance to encounter other lives and other
points of view via the language of the imagination.